OTHER BOOKS BY MALCOLM ...

Of Land Sea And Sky – The Autobiography Of An Adventurer and Entrepreneur

Hill's Heroes Volume 1 – A collection of short biographies of Napoleon Hill's heroes from his iconic book Think And Grow Rich. People who changed their world and still affect our lives today.

How To Anchor Safely – So You Sleep Well
A guide to anchoring a yacht or motorboat for people who intend to liveaboard and spend a lot of time at anchor in order to save money or explore more remote places or both.

How To Buy A Boat For The Liveaboard Lifestyle
Based upon the experience of buying and then living aboard a Dutch Steel Cutter Ketch for ten years, and travelling widely, this book examines the attributes necessary, and pros and cons of different types of boat, construction, rig and equipment needed for this lifestyle.

THE NEXT BOOK IS INTENDED TO BE ANOTHER NOVEL, TO BE ENTITLED 'MY FRIEND SCIPIO'

CONTENTS

Chapter 1 – Lord Have Mercy On My Soul	4
Chapter 2 – A Chance Discovery	8
Chapter 3 – Of Curiosity And Cats	13
Chapter 4 – A Minor Upheaval	30
Chapter 5 – A New Life	36
Chapter 6 – A Question Of Diplomacy	50
Chapter 7 – Old Fashioned Police Work	55
Chapter 8 – The First Breakthrough	64
Chapter 9 – Tanya	69
Chapter 10 – Decision Time Again	72
Chapter 11 – A Chance Encounter	77
Chapter 12 – Sturgis	86
Chapter 13 – Back On The Road Again	99
Chapter 14 – San Francisco	112
Chapter 15 – Manhunt	122
Chapter 16 – A Small War In Central America	136
Chapter 17 – The Winds Of Change	139
Chapter 18 – The Making Of Tanya	152
Chapter 19 – A Question Of Conscience	160
Chapter 20 – Bear Traps	165
Chapter 21 – Hobbs And Donohue	171
Chapter 22 – Reporters	178
Chapter 23 – The Cat Has Nine Lives	183
Chapter 24 – Who Goes Where	189
Chapter 25 – No Loose Ends	195
Chapter 26 – The Italian Job	203
Epilogue	204
Disclaimer	206
Glossary and acknowledgements	207

For Kathy Rohn

TIGHTROPE

CHAPTER ONE - LORD HAVE MERCY ON MY SOUL

The Catholic hospice of the Sacred Heart near Catania is set half way up the side of a valley in stunning mountains that keep it cool even in the height of the Sicilian summer, secluded and quiet if a little brown in July and August. It looks out across an olive grove that might have been there since Roman times the trees are so old, divided and gnarled although probably only three or four hundred years old in reality. The scent of wild lavender airily drifts through the netted but permanently open, in summer, dormitory bedroom windows. All is serene, tranquil and as beautiful as anywhere Europe has to offer.

Or boring beyond belief if you're a young nurse with few distractions. Deathbed confessions have become a way of enlivening a testing way of life for some of the younger nurses lacking the self sacrificial religious convictions of their colleagues in holy orders. 'There just aren't enough novices these days' laments Mother Superior to herself as she patrols the corridors, but the church is doing fine financially and can afford to employ nurses, cleaners and caretakers, 'Our Lord will always provide'.

Tanya, now old and very frail, both in appearance and in fact, is on her deathbed and making her last confession to Father Egidio. The doctors can find nothing specific that is physically wrong with her other than extreme old age and a clear desire, now, to pass on. She is entirely rational, has all her mental faculties and a good memory, but she is ready to go. Nurse Carmella strains at the door trying desperately to hear, without being seen. Sadly it won't make for good tittle tattle, in fact apart from confessing she's been faithful to one man her entire life, not exactly a confession at all in Carmella's opinion, the rest of Tanya's lucid but quietly spoken words, such as Carmella can hear, make little or no sense whatsoever.

"Mike was the only man I ever loved, the only man I ever slept with in my entire life, tell me Father, I will find him again now, won't I, beyond this life, surely soulmates will find one another again?"

Father Egidio tries to reassure her in the most non committal way he can, talking about the day when all will be raised from the dead, despite having more than a few doubts about his own faith, and himself wondering, not to say doubting, whether there really is anything more to come after this earthly life. However, his curiosity has bested him and he can't resist asking one last question about the strange story she's already told him. Half of which Carmella arrived too late to hear.

Tanya appears to the priest to be re-living some past experience, as if in a trance and yet seemingly at peace with everything and everyone; does your life flash before you Father Egidio wondered. Finally Tanya is speaking freely, more freely than she has done in more than three decades.

"We didn't trust them you see, neither Government, we knew we couldn't really touch the compensation, just initially Mike said, we'll use it just once or twice to get us started, then we'll put it out of our minds forever, otherwise the withdrawals will allow them to find us very easily and they will kill us I believe, probably sooner rather than later."

With her final breath Tanya whispers.

"Mike, forgive me my darling I've kept you waiting, but I'm coming now".

Carmella surreptitiously tip toes away. Knowing better than to even think to interrogate Father, she seeks out her best friend Liberata at lunchtime.

"Well, anything interesting cara?"

"She was faithful to one man all her life, not the sort of thing you lie about on your deathbed is it? So no, nothing exciting there, but the two of them were mixed up in some sort of criminal activity and it went very high it seems, government stuff, defence even, but then I thought she said they robbed a bank, which isn't easy but it's not a matter for the government. Then she prattled on about the Ndrangheta getting the blame for it. No, made no sense at all. It was probably the morphine talking."

"Oh well Marisa won't be with us long and I bet she's lived a bit!"

"Yes, but if Tanya was once a big time crook I'd love to know, wouldn't you?"

"No one is going to tell the likes of us, so you might as well forget about it."

"I suppose you're right but life is so dull here, just imagine who we could have been looking after without knowing it, a mafia boss, a spy, a jewel thief, Oh God I wish I knew."

"Did I just hear you take our Lord's name in vain Carmella? Back to work now the pair of you and less of this chiacchiere and don't let me catch either of you two eavesdropping either, I don't know exactly what you were talking about, but it sounds a bit suspect to me and I'm not entirely pazza yet."

" Sorry mother."

In his office, back in his own wing Father Egidio found himself pondering the morality and ethics of accepting a somewhat problematical bequest. After all the confessional is the confessional, he cannot break the confidence, cannot tell anyone, least of all the bank or the authorities. This cross he must carry alone, and then again, money is after all money, it enables good works, even if he is no longer sure it is actually His work.

CHAPTER TWO - A CHANCE DISCOVERY

John Baird, no relation to John Logie Baird is retired. Balding but sprightly, and fit enough to play tennis once a week in the village, he has, inspired by his illustrious namesake, spent most of his working life at Marconi Electronics. He knew people who'd been involved in World War Two military research at Marconi for the SOE and later MI5 and 6.

Although his own work had mostly concerned radio communication, long wave, shortwave, very high frequency, single sideband, you name it and a bit on radar too, he had occasionally been asked personally by the security services about range, detection, interception and suchlike. He is still in fact a walking encyclopedia, but the technology has moved on, left him behind. Miniaturization, digitisation, have made him an animal of the past if not quite a dinosaur yet.

Largely forgotten by his younger colleagues and with his older mentors mostly deceased, John, now retired, spends much of his time in the shed at the bottom of his garden. An extension lead provides power and he has a work bench with a soldering iron and an array of testing equipment, mostly with old fashioned dials, meters and so on, plus some new-fangled digital stuff. There is an array of drawers carefully labelled containing his treasures, every type of electrical component from resistors and capacitors, to fuses, connectors, screws, insulation materials, wire, magnets, electric motors, dynamos, magnetos, headphones, microphones and much more.

A large and very tall roof mounted aerial outside also gives away the fact that John is a ham radio enthusiast. Just occasionally he picks up single sideband communications from yachts in mid Atlantic and is able to help with weather advice or routing to try and avoid the worst storms. Once he even relayed an SOS to the coastguard at Falmouth.

His wife Jean of thirty three, mostly very happy, years readily accepts his obsession, they have a strong marriage and John's hobby prevents him getting under her feet. In fact she'd been secretly dreading his retirement. In the event it worked out rather to her liking, she could still have the church ladies round for a chat and a coffee, she prided herself on her real coffee, John would be in the shed, she'd take a cup down the garden for him, before getting on with the serious business of finding out what the vicar's latest escapades had involved and with whom.

She could go walking with Sue and Elisabeth, John would be in the shed and wouldn't even notice. Jean would take him a coffee before they set off, just to be sure he wouldn't be asking for one in the forty minutes it would take them to walk around the new estate. During which they would have the usual moan about the architecture, discuss the likely value of their own homes, in light of the extortionate prices being charged for these new little boxes.

They would also talk about the wickedness of developers who were now selling detached houses leasehold with multiple restrictions written in, when in the opinion of all three ladies they really ought to be freehold. The purchasers should be free to change the windows, or do whatever they wanted with walls and gardens and so on. After all they cost enough. Time the government did something about it. Same old comfortable conversation happily repeated and occasionally interspersed with some news about sons, daughters, grandchildren and holiday plans.

She could go to art on Tuesdays, Pilates on Thursdays and Aqua aerobics on Fridays. On Wednesday mornings they both played tennis with the other retirees in the village.

Some things had changed of course, the addition of tennis to their routine and doing it together was a definite plus, not something they could have considered before he retired and there had been a suggestion of badminton in the winter evenings too. Other things had changed, that were not for the better, but, nothing she couldn't cope with.

When John had been working he'd been very good at not bringing his work back home with him. In fact in the last few years he'd mostly come home tired and bored with no mention of work required. They'd eat together then snuggle up on the settee to watch the latest box set, or Scandi or Euro drama. Very satisfactory; occasionally, if there was nothing good on they'd even go to bed with a good book and read to one another, his choice, her choice, all very diplomatic and easy going.

Since John had retired he'd once more become the captain of his own soul, made his own decisions about what to work on in his little paradise at the bottom of the garden and had found a new lease on life. She could hardly begrudge him that.

However, it did rankle when she'd cooked a lovely meal to order, one that he'd said he'd been dying for, and now, when she yelled at the shed "dinner's ready", she'd get the "just a moment dear" response, that she was becoming all too used to. Only to be kept waiting half an hour, or very occasionally more, for him to appear.

As with so many fundamentally good relationships any small thing that annoys tends to grow in importance. Jean was almost beginning to think she could cope with a drunken womanising bastard if only he'd be there for dinner on time. She knew in her heart this was tosh and nonsense, but, nonetheless the annoyance was multiplying like a cancer in her mind.

John meanwhile found himself working enthusiastically on his new pet theory, well not even that really, just a thought to pass some time in fact, a thought that said if electrical currents can interfere with radio signals, so radio signals should, just maybe, disrupt electrical currents, and if so, could that serve a useful purpose? It was not something serious, he didn't truly believe in what he was looking for himself, it had become more of a game in fact.

Initially he set up an experiment with a small transmitter in the shed, next to a light bulb, with a new, super sensitive current meter in the circuit. He had no expectation that he could alter the intensity of the light, but wondered if his new fangled sensitive meter might possibly reveal slight differences in the current, caused by interference as he varied the frequency and strength of the radio waves.

The radio was powered from the mains, the rest from a battery, therefore altering the power of the transmitter would in no way interfere with the other circuit directly. Frustrated that there is no effect, although not surprised, he hooks up his powerful single sideband transmitter and plugs the indoor aerial into that.

Whilst very slowly turning the dials in the more extreme frequency ranges he suddenly freezes and falls back in his chair, his head lolling to one side, neither has the light flickered nor the meter blinked and yet the infinitesimal electrical impulses in his brain are confused. Automatic motor functions such as breathing continue, but the tiny electrical impulses that send messages to his limbs are disabled, he cannot move or think clearly.

From up near the house comes the cry "Dinner!".
He's unable to reply or move. After 50 minutes without so much as an excuse from the garden Jean loses her temper for the first time in their long marriage. Angry as hell, in her own mind at least, she becomes a fire breathing, sword wielding virago, 'damn him and to hell with the consequences for whatever he thinks he's working on' she thinks to herself as she pulls out the plug on his precious power cable.

She will soon regret her anger and her actions and remorsefully turn back into something more reminiscent of her usual angel of mercy persona, but unbeknownst to her at that moment of pure fury, she possibly saved the dear man from any real and lasting damage.

Shortly afterwards John staggers up to the house, white and shaking, but already working out what has happened to him and what it all means, as Jean insists he really should go to A and E, something he flatly refuses to do.

CHAPTER THREE - OF CURIOSITY AND CATS

The clatter of the overworked diesel engine died away and the driver sat motionless, breathing deeply and allowing the roaring calm, left behind, to sweep over him. For a while he was almost too tired to get out of the cab. It had been a good night's work though. December usually meant lots of theatre goers and parties, and the crowds would increase exponentially towards Christmas and the millennium. Not that he intended working that particular night, the potential for drunks and disasters was just too great.

Still that didn't matter, tonight at least, he'd cleared over £380 between leaving home at 4pm yesterday and now, almost 3:30am. Although the last fare hadn't been exactly in the Romford direction, at least Hampstead was near enough to the, thankfully, newly improved North Circular Road, that he could make good time getting home.

When he had pulled up outside the attractive, upper middle class, five bedroom, detached tudor style house, a beautiful woman had leaned out of the window in her nightie and loudly heckled her husband who was in the act of paying the fare.

"James this has to stop, it's Natalie's birthday, she's only five for goodness sake, she fought off the tiredness for as long as she could, then cried herself to sleep, for goodness sake her birthday is only once a year..."

"I'm sorry Suzy, truly I am, they called a sudden meeting about this new thing, look I can't talk in the street." He hurried into the house. The tip, probably accidentally, was enormous.

The taxi driver, after pulling up outside his home, knew that however tired he felt now, he wouldn't be able to sleep until he'd checked the cash, wound down slowly, had a cup of tea and maybe watched a bit of desperate late night TV. He found himself mulling these things over as he psyched himself up to drag himself out of the driving seat.

Just why, or how the small, dark case in the back caught his eye in the deep gloom, he would come to wonder often in the next couple of years. Working the hours that he did had certainly done no harm to his night vision. In fact it had seemingly improved, which on this occasion was no blessing. Almost automatically he opened the back of the cab and grabbed the handle, before trudging through the broken gate and up the overgrown path. He stepped on the pile of bricks that made do for a front step and opened the white UPVC door. Michael O'Brien lived alone.

The generally sensible, conservative, even cautious Mr Michael O'Brien, he who took no chances, even with drunks at New Year had inadvertently made the biggest mistake of the rest of his life. Innocently enough, he would tell himself in the future, when trying to look on the brighter side, or boost a sagging self confidence.

Chances are, he told himself, if he'd just left it on the back seat they'd simply have broken into the cab, taken what they wanted and assumed he'd never seen it. Which he wouldn't have done if he'd left it there, but having seen it, it seemed natural to just pick it up. In the not very far off future he would heartily wish that he hadn't seen it.

'Boredom makes you do things you might not otherwise do' he thought and after a cup of tea he decided to be nosy. Truth be told the wife of his last fare was pretty spectacular looking and he just couldn't help himself. The acronym MILF came to mind. The exchange between husband and wife in the street would prove very helpful.

After quite a lot of playing around with physical locks and then passwords; he'd experimented with James, Suzy, Susie, Natalie, the kiddie's date of birth, the street name and number where he'd dropped his fare and various combinations of all of them, suddenly he was in. Only to find the words Top Secret staring out at him from the screen of the laptop.

Well it was too corny to be real. Must be a hoax. One of the boys on the rank had set him up. Besides, if he could get into it with his limited knowledge of computers, then it couldn't be the real McCoy, could it?

Nonetheless, it felt, and looked all too real, he wasn't really sure he ought to look further. He had picked up the fare close enough to Whitehall, and the guy did have a military bearing about him. You got to know a lot of types of people, if not actually a lot of people, as a London cabbie. Yes, he had definitely been military, or police; intelligence services? Even that was possible.

Mike turned the TV on while he considered what to do. Choices, religious debate, 'no'. Music that might have meant something to him if he'd been twenty years younger, 'I think not'. Bought in American quiz show, 'give me a break'. Ice hockey, 'for goodness sake' and of course at this time in the morning there was usually some so called adult entertainment.

Slightly grainy reception in Romford, but it kept him from thinking about what he missed most, or maybe it was just a poor substitute. He knew he wouldn't really enjoy it that much. Terrestrial porn was more than a little limited and the poor quality reception certainly didn't help. On the other hand the large breasted, raven haired beauty conducting the threesome with her slim suntanned friend and boyfriend, seemingly for the benefit of the peeping tom next door, was at least amusing even if it was a somewhat dated 'Confessions Of', kind of a low budget movie.

He kept it on for some time. Despite the contrived scenario, women playing with other women was always something of a turn on, even if it was only the fondling of breasts and sucking of nipples that typified soft core and never got below the waist. He thought momentarily about calling Rachel, but it had been his idea to work these hours and see her only at weekends. So there was no one else to blame when he felt horny and there was no-one around to screw or even just cuddle.

Ultimately he preferred it that way, sex on tap had a downside. While sex with the rampant, broad minded Rachel, after five days apart, was always good, fucking good actually. He felt more sort of faithful, imagining what he would do to Rachel, whilst actually enjoying the visual stimulation of keeping one eye on those admittedly fabulous, apparently natural silicone free, breasts now flowing to and fro on the screen as the boyfriend joined in with sufficient enthusiasm, that he just might not have been wholly acting. Trouble with those movies is the creators seemed to think there was a need for comedy and their own story line to interfere with his sexual fantasies.

Mike turned it off and imagined smacking Rachel's arse. Hard. He'd thought himself pretty experienced when he met her, but he'd never actually smacked a woman before, in fact it was something he never thought he would do. He'd been surprised to say the least, when after removing her clothes, and she his for the first time, on their second date, she had immediately said "you can smack me if you like". At least he wasn't so naïve that he didn't realise it was a request, an instruction even, rather than merely a suggestion.

He'd been hesitant at first but her reaction was.

"If you're going to smack me, try and make it real!"

Mike thought of himself as both gentleman and as a considerate lover, so whatever Rachel wanted, Rachel got, she was happy to cater to all his wants too, they had a great sex life, even if it was weekends only.

Half imagining and half remembering, what he would and had previously done with Rachel, whilst guiltily superimposing in his mind the image of the porn star lately on the screen, all thoughts of work, lost property and how tired he felt had fled. By now the movie would have reached its fake climax, as he reached his own and leant over for a tissue, pondering once more what to do with the laptop. Little knowing he'd never see Rachel again, ever.

The options were a trip to Hampstead next day to return it, drop it off at the carriage office, which was the official and correct thing to do and what he would have done if he hadn't hacked it and seen what he'd seen. Another possibility was to maybe just destroy the thing, deny all knowledge if asked and then forget it.

Or was there another? What about the media? If it was genuine, and if it was important there could be a lot of money in it. He didn't want to feel like a traitor, but then, he considered, he had never even read, let alone signed the official secrets act. Not normally a requirement for cabbing, he chuckled to himself and this might be his only opportunity, that once in a lifetime thing that would lead to a large windfall, and if the payout was large enough it didn't even matter if he lost his licence.

His tired thinking became muddled. He would feel a traitor if it turned out to be something of national importance. If it wasn't important it wouldn't be worth money. He thought about his earning potential as a cabby and his actual desires and aspirations. He thought about the moral implications of nuclear and germ warfare. His imagination ran riot, though his imaginings never in fact got close to the information the computer actually contained.

Ultimately he decided that a decision was impossible unless he actually looked at whatever the damn thing had in it. Hand it back and 'they', whoever 'they' were, were bound to want to know if he'd got in, and he, almost superstitiously, believed there would be some safeguard that could tell them that he had got in, and certainly at the very least, that he'd opened some sort of file, which he already had. So the damage had been done anyway. Now, feeling very naïve, he went back to the computer and started to look at the pages which followed the intriguing warning on the 'Top Secret' cover page.

The introductory text made him sit up straight, as fully awake as a shot of adrenaline might have made him. The documents held details of a device, which emitted a wave (radio he assumed although it could have been sound for all he knew) of a frequency, which, when broadcast powerfully enough would paralyse all human activity. Not the automatic functions like breathing, but disable the conscious mind, so that those within range would simply stop doing anything, their brains unable to send signals to their limbs.

A brain jamming device if you like. Of course there would be casualties, road, rail and air accidents would be inevitable, the text explained, if the device were used on a large scale. Surgeons would simply freeze in mid operation and so on. However, on a battlefield, an army could be stopped and disarmed with virtually no difficulty, and virtually no loss of life. Ships could be prevented from firing missiles, possibly even submarines could be disabled.

One's own troops need only wear receivers which would pick up a counter signal, a sort of antidote wave if you like and the receivers themselves could even double as communication devices. Is there no end to human creativity when it comes to warfare he thought, so sad that such brilliance, as he saw it, totally unaware that it was an entirely accidental discovery, couldn't be put to better use. Nonetheless, the idea of an army in Sony Walkmans appealed to his sense of the ridiculous. And, although much of the scientific jargon, abbreviations and symbols went straight over his head, the implications did not!

Of course, should the technology, or even just the knowledge become widely available, as the document needlessly spelled out to him, then all international advantage would be lost. Should it fall into criminal hands, then the cost of protecting banks, building societies, supermarkets et al would be vast. Not to mention equipping police forces and essential services with 'antidote' signal receivers to accept and boost the cancellation wave which would have to be broadcast in the appropriate time and place.

As Mike scrolled through, so the pages became even more detailed and technical. On the one hand after doing 'the knowledge' as the London cabbies' training and exam course is affectionately known, he had developed an extremely good memory for detail, on the other hand the science meant very little to him. Now the effects of the shock were wearing off and he began to feel incredibly sleepy. As if in a trance he turned the laptop off, put it on the floor, superstitiously wiped the keyboard with his handkerchief, closed the screen down, trudged upstairs, cleaned his teeth, stripped and fell into bed.

Expertly, and almost silently, his front door lock was picked, the small extra bolt and chain cut, with something very sophisticated, quiet and quick. Although Mike was so deeply asleep they could have used an angle grinder. It would be days anyway before the local constabulary would even begin trying to assess what had taken place and visually all would look entirely normal on the outside of the former council house. Three darkly dressed figures slipped inside. A pad was held to Mike's face and seconds later a needle was inserted into his upper arm. His dreams may have been troubled slightly, but to all intents and purposes Mike O'Brien slumbered serenely on.

When he awoke, it would be to very strange surroundings indeed. He would still be flat on his back, but with hands and arms firmly secured and in a blackness so impenetrable he would wonder momentarily if he'd woken at all.

That event was still several hours hence, as he was first driven to a remote house, some two hours away, near a quiet Cambridgeshire village. The kind where all the residents firmly believed they knew everything that went on in the parish.

As Mike opened his eyes, comprehended that he could see nothing at all, nor move any part of his anatomy, his first instinct was to doubt his own sanity. He didn't want to admit to himself that it hadn't been a dream, and yet, unless he was still dreaming, he was in some sort of living, full on, wide awake nightmare.

He sighed, and was greeted by a strange voice in the blackness, "awake at last then my friend". Why did the innocent expression "my friend" always sound so sinister? It was meant to of course, but if there was any justice in the world those two simple words would be incapable of such corruption. When he had got in last night and later read through that fateful file, his mind had wandered in a similar way through sheer fatigue. Now, powerful drugs were playing with his thought processes.

Unfortunately, the mind of a London cabbie, one long used to daydreaming and at the same time keeping up a degree of spacial awareness and concentration, was not about to respond in the same way as another might, even a mind trained to resist interrogation. A result that would lead the interrogator to the erroneous conclusion that the mind in question was in fact superbly trained to resist interrogation.

Ultimately, in fact, to convince him that the seemingly ordinary Mr O'Brien was actually anything but ordinary. A conclusion which, if taken at face value was not too far wide of the mark, certainly in Mike O'Brien's opinion anyway. However, the idea that Mr O'Brien was a highly trained spy was astonishingly wide of the mark.

Nonetheless, that is the conclusion the CIA man, with the intentionally misleading, phoney eastern European, slightly Russian sounding accent had reached. After some days of non-stop, round the houses discussions, in the dark, in the bright lights, sleep deprived, all the simple conventional techniques Mr CIA was left quite unsure as to just how much Mr O'B really new, or understood of the technology, why the British officer had passed him the laptop in the first place and most importantly, for whom Mr bloody O'Brien and the MI5 officer he could not interrogate for political reasons, were working.

What he was pretty convinced of was Mr O'Brien's skill in not revealing the answers, in short his skill as a field operative. He wasn't prepared, or allowed to use torture, even waterboarding, just drugs, those without too many harmful long term effects, so far as the USA acknowledged anyway, on a citizen of an ally and on that ally's own soil too, so he'd have to rely on the devious. Plan B.

Accepting the obvious, and silently thanking the Limeys for another brilliant invention, which the US could benefit from now, and take the credit for historically, did not enter into the mind of this tunnel-visioned US patriot and certainly didn't suit his perception of the big picture for the 21st Century.

When Mr O'Brien escaped, he would be even more convinced of his status as a top class spook. Of course they would first have to give him that window of opportunity, but if he took it, coldly and efficiently, despite suspecting he was meant to, yet without any other viable course of action, then this must be a highly trained, daring, experienced and resourceful man.

Let the opportunity go and he might be just what he appeared to be, a London cabbie in the wrong place at the wrong time. As with the dunking stool witch trials of the middle ages though, innocence would also prove to be a death sentence. Regrettably there was no other way. Funny he thought, that he hadn't been authorised to use torture and yet an execution and cover up would almost certainly be just fine. Just a London taxi driver who'd disappeared, no real clues why or where, a file that would remain open but gather dust until it was forgotten entirely.

The lights went on. Mike was given good food, clothes (his own, brought from Romford that first night) and the freedom of a lavishly furnished country house living room and most importantly a bathroom with a large and deep bath as well as a shower. He figured they were going for the good cop bad cop thing, or trying the carrot after the stick, so, without much optimism, he looked around for an opportunity to leg it.

The windows were impenetrable, there was an armed man outside the door. His meals were delivered by another man, the bulge under his jacket indicating that he too carried a weapon. The bathroom and toilet were next door, he had only to ask. On the one and only occasion that he heard the toilet door close, just before the arrival of his food, Mike gambled that the guard was taking a leak and took his opportunity for flight, just as his captors thought he might.

Feeling as though he were in an Errol Flynn movie (who can say where the effect of the now discontinued drugs left off and his own peculiar thought process took over), from behind the door he smashed an expensive looking vase over the head of the man with the lunch tray, having first wrapped it in a cushion cover to deaden the noise and prevent pieces clattering to the floor.

Revelling in his own initiative, he removed the fellow's jacket, took the gun from the holster and then used the holster straps to secure the 'waiter's' hands behind his back. He then shoved two whole sandwiches into the man's mouth. Thinking that he might more easily get out if he looked like one of them from a distance, he took off his jeans and shoes and put on the waiter's black trousers, and brogues. He then used the curtain lanyard to tie the man's feet to the radiator. He shoved the gun barrel down the back of his own trousers' waistband, what was the use of going to the movies otherwise he thought, although he'd never fired a gun, didn't have time to examine it, or see if there was a safety catch and didn't really expect he would ever use it. Still it was one less barrel to be pointed at him.

He was immensely proud of his achievements, so much so, that all hint of nerves left him, like a jittery actor who has just stepped on to the stage and immersed himself in character. He slipped on the jacket and stole carefully out of the house. The occupant of the loo emerged to watch his back disappear around the corner of the corridor. All the while he was being watched by hidden cameras anyhow and his captors were confident he would not elude them, simply lead them to his employers or those commanding or handling him.

Outside for the first time in days, he found himself in the grounds of a large country house. There was a long drive sloping away, towards gates about two hundred yards away. The drive was straight. There was a parked car pointing down the slope, it wasn't locked, but being an honest chap, Mr O'Brien had no idea how to hot-wire it. The alarm would be raised any second now by the guy in the loo he figured. An idea came to him. Quickly he let the handbrake off and pushed the car hard down the drive as a decoy then sprinted fifty yards across the lawn to some trees. Before long he came to a wire fence with razor wire at the top.

Electrified, alarmed? He had no idea. He followed it for a while then found a spot where something had burrowed under. Fox, badger? Whatever it was, it could hardly have got under without touching the wire mesh and since there was no corpse QED it was safe. He found a fallen bough and using it as a lever, enlarged the gap and scrambled through. Now he felt less like Errol Flynn or James Bond and more like Peter Rabbit. Whatever, he was free, wherever that might be, but for how long?

Confident he could keep a general sense of direction, he'd been doing it long enough, and at least go straight, he set off assuming he would find a road. At first he ran, complimenting himself that swimming every morning and cycling at other times had kept him reasonably fit, at least for a man who spent the rest of his day sitting on it.

Back at the house, the CIA officer in charge was fairly relaxed, this was what he'd expected for the most part and planned on, there was the issue of the gun though. They wouldn't be haring after the car, the security cameras had witnessed that bit of nonsense, but still he misinterpreted it, putting it down more to the desperation of a man who knew he was following a script, than to naivety or amateurism. And there was the tracking device.

"Where did you put it Jim?"

"In his shoe."

"My god he changed fucking shoes with Bob".

"How could he know?"

"I don't suppose he did know, he's just fucking lucky, a fucking good actor and fucking good at what he does."

"So get the fuck on his tail will you and be careful, he's armed now, what genius went in with a gun on him eh. Bob"

'No transponder, and now the bastard is armed' which meant they'd have to be careful how they approached him in future. He suddenly began to feel just a little bit jinxed and under pressure. All that swearing meant the bastard had got to him, not the other way round. Still it was a minor hiccup, basically it was going to plan and he had good guys working for him. O'Brien would reveal what they wanted to know, he was sure of that at least, just as long as they didn't lose him.

Anticipating a road sooner or later, Mike was in fact confronted with another fence, but no razor wire this time. Although there was no sound of pursuit yet, he'd seen enough movies to figure he'd better not hang around and hauled himself over it, not quite SAS style but adequate. The ground dropped sharply away and he half fell, half slid into a railway cutting.

If he was followed this far, then unless they had dogs, they'd now have to split up he figured. He didn't know how many there'd be, but at least three he guessed, so that meant one left, one right and one up the opposite bank. He turned left and sprinted. He wasn't leaving footprints, making a noise or smashing through the undergrowth, but after about fifty yards, it dawned on him that he was pretty visible to anyone looking straight down the track. He kept to his direction, one way was as good as another, but took to the scrub at the side, it was slower but less obvious.

In fact his instincts were exactly right. Three men had followed him and they had split up at the railway. The man coming in Mike's direction kept to the track, and despite the distance and the amount of running he'd done, he was not in the least bit out of breath. Mike on the other hand was suffering a little, he could see a platform not more than three hundred yards further on. There was no guarantee that would offer any safety, even if there was a snowballs chance of getting there unseen. Having glimpsed his pursuer, but as yet unseen himself, he lay down in the longest grass, behind the largest bushes he could see and tried not to move a muscle, or even breathe.

Thank God for Railtrack priorities and the cost of clearing overgrown embankments. His pursuer stopped, on the track, just a few feet below him and pulled out a radio.

"Sir I'm almost at Dullingham Station, I don't think he can have come this way, you guys got anything?"

"Nothing here, if he turned right, made it to the level crossing and picked up a ride straight away, he could be in Newmarket, Sawston, or even be on the M11 by now. I wish we still had dogs instead of microchips! Bob, you got anything?"

"Nothing sir."

"OK back to the house Bob, Jim, you check out the station. If there's anyone there see if they saw him, impersonate a copper if you have to, then get back to the house and we'll decide on our next move."

Mike watched the man trot easily up to the platform and disappear. He'd only heard one side of the conversation, so he stayed put for nearly half an hour. Then, when there was no sign of anyone he continued, somewhat cautiously to the station. His pursuer must have returned via the road.

The station was empty and unmanned, there was a ticket machine, but his luck hadn't extended to finding a wallet full of cash in the jacket. Nor did he want to hang around for a train, and, not knowing who, or what organisation was after him, he didn't want any contact with the police, for all that his interrogators had sounded Russian. The police would think he was a nutter anyway with a story like that and instead of believing him would probably arrest him for carrying a gun. He thought about ditching it but on balance decided not yet.

He made his way outside to the road and started walking. The name Dullingham meant nothing to him. After a few miles he came to the A1304, Newmarket one way and M11 south the other. He suddenly felt optimistic and although the southerly direction was probably the one they'd expect him to take, he decided to gamble.

His impressions of his captors led him to believe they were neither British nor legit so he doubted there'd be anything like roadblocks, for them it would be like looking for a needle in a haystack. The tables were starting to turn, largely on the one piece of luck, his decision to swap shoes. Not knowing that, he felt pretty pleased with himself, more so as a lorry responded to his thumb, pulled over and the driver asked where he was going.

"Tunbridge Wells"

The truck driver asked him if the party season was getting too much for him already. For the first time he thought about his appearance. Unshaven, black trousers, black jacket and black shoes, with a white t-shirt – somewhat off white now. Indeed he must look like a refugee from a party that had got a bit out of hand. He stuck with that story, embellished it a bit, feigned a hangover and asked the driver if he minded him getting some shut-eye. When he'd given his destination as Tunbridge Wells the driver had said he could drop him at the Dartford Service Area.

"You'll easily get a lift on from there mate" he'd said.

Now his response was disappointed in tone but accepting "OK I'll wake you up at Dartford, I'd figured on a bit of company, but what the hell, you look like death, best sleep it off".

He would have liked to have bought the driver a coffee, but his fictitious friends had left him penniless in the middle of nowhere for a prank after the celebrations. So at least he'd offered an explanation. At Dartford he made a reverse charge call to Tunbridge Wells and forty minutes later his real best friend was collecting him.

CHAPTER FOUR - A MINOR UPHEAVAL

His other 'friends' from the CIA had, unknowingly, overtaken him on the M11, on their way to Romford to turn the house over for clues where they were to find an address book, that would include his current destination. He knew a lot of people though and by the time they investigated the address in Tunbridge Wells he'd be well on his way again. Close calls which none of the players involved were ever aware of.

Unaware also, that his address book was being interrogated, all Mike O'Brien wanted was another bath, a shave and someone to discuss his predicament with. Someone he could trust. There were two guys he could turn to for help. Dave or Martin. Tunbridge Wells was a sight closer than Glasgow, so Dave it was.

He left out the contents of the dossier, in the vague hope that by doing so he would protect his friend. The rest of the story he spilled to Dave at the same time as shaving, bathing and borrowing some jeans, new t-shirt, underwear and trainers.

"Basically Dave I'm bricking it. I don't want to go to the police, just in case it's our lot that are doing this, even though I think that's unlikely, but if it is some foreign agency or criminal organisation, then the authorities may want to use me as bait. Basically it's all too big for me, I just want out of it, now".

"Well, getting out might not be the easiest thing, and I think in your shoes I personally would go to the police. I'd be more worried about them taking it seriously though. That gun would make them sit up, but from what I know of the police they'd go for the easy collar rather than worry about the whole truth, so you'd have to lose it and then your story would sound bonkers. Of course I believe you. If I was in some horrible situation I'd want you to take it seriously. So I have a suggestion for you. You look a bit like me and you don't want to be going home.

"Take my passport, get your hair cut like mine in the picture, I can give you the leather jacket I was wearing when it was taken which will help, then you can take my drivers licence and credit cards and get the hell out. They only glance at the pictures anyway. I suggest you go to the States or Canada. In fact if you fancy the States, then go via Canada, immigration is less strict into Canada and passport control on the border between the two is more relaxed than at the major airports.

"Take a long break, you can give me a letter with power of attorney over your affairs and I'll try to get your mortgage frozen and do whatever else I can. Give me the name and address of your solicitor too, that might be useful, although I've no idea what the system will allow me to do. Now look I'm not made of money, so I'll report my cards lost or stolen in two weeks and get new ones. Use them for your ticket and as sparingly as you can for those two weeks, then cut them up, get rid of them and you're on your own OK."

"What about this" Mike said pulling out the pistol.

"Well you can't take it to an airport and if either of us hands it in there'll be impossible questions to answer, they'll probably trace the owner but if they do, then that could make things worse, or better depending who it is, but no point anyway unless you're going to change your mind and spill the whole story. I suggest I spray it with WD, put it in a couple of plastic bags and bury it in the back garden as an insurance policy in case the truth ever does need to come out."

"You're a bloody star Dave."

And so it was that the very next day Mike O'Brien was half way across the Atlantic to Canada, en route to the USA. A country he'd been to before, where he could enjoy the climate, speak the language, probably get casual work and as he thought, where he'd be half a world away from the man with the eastern European, Ukrainian, Russian, whatever it was, accent!

He passed through immigration at Montreal with hardly a glance and a cheery "enjoy your vacation Mr Harrison", a comment which nearly saw him lose his composure, but no one was suspicious and tourists brought in a lot of foreign revenue, even the officials tended to be friendly in Canada.

At the airport he used Dave's cards to get $200 Canadian and $500 American, then found himself a room for the night. At the hotel he made various enquiries, got himself a map and later, after mulling it over, he booked a taxi for the morning that would take him to the bus station. That evening he had a steak and all the trimmings. He positioned himself in the hotel coffee shop in such a way that he could see everyone who came in. No one looked at all threatening, or remotely interested in him. He didn't expect there to be, but was also reassured to find there was nothing on CNN about security breaches, secret weapons, or missing taxi driver spies. He slept soundly.

In the morning he had a typical North American breakfast, pancakes, eggs over easy and crispy bacon with plenty of coffee. He was getting into the lifestyle already and felt ready to take on the world. He had planned to use Dave's VISA card one more time to buy a Greyhound Lines Ameripass, which would provide access to buses throughout the USA and much of Canada.

However, it occurred to him that if anyone found out he was using that particular card they could already track him to Montreal and the hotel had taken an old style paper and carbon imprint of the card for security.

He used the card to get another $500 Canadian, caught his taxi to the bus station paying cash to the hotel after telling them not to process the credit card and retrieving the paper slip, then he paid cash for his bus pass too. He'd thought about asking the taxi driver not to tell anyone who might ask, where he had taken him, but figured that would only make him more memorable. He tried not to chat with the taxi driver, just confirmed he was on vacation, no name, no pack drill.

If he said nothing he'd soon be forgotten, there must be plenty of other foreigners passing in and out of the yellow cab. He expressly did not enter into a conversation about life as a taxi driver in the UK, as he would have, had he truly been on 'vacation', as they say on the North American continent he'd realised. In fact rather than saying something he'd later regret he said next to nothing, just gazed out of the window like the majority of tourists.

The first leg of his journey was to New York. The bus would be crowded and the border crossing was likely to be even more hurried under those circumstances he hoped. It was as he wished. Immigration control into Canada was recognised by the USA, the border more or less a formality, he was home and dry.

At least that was how it felt. Everything seemed to be so easy and going so well. Given that his whole life was turned upside down of course. However, he figured he was in his second country since fleeing and making a passable stab at covering his tracks. At the first rest stop he destroyed the credit cards and the paper slip. He didn't want to be tempted to use the cards further for two reasons. One, he didn't want to take advantage of his benefactor any more than he had to and two he was still worried that they might be a route by which he could be found. At the first bank he encountered he changed his remaining Canadian dollars into American. He was left with about 650 bucks. He was endeavouring to get into the US vernacular, but couldn't see being able to pull off the accent for a long time to come, if ever.

The bus was comfortable, warm and there was even a bit of legroom. He could doze when necessary and although a couple of people passed the time of day, he was merely polite, without encouraging conversation and was largely left to his own devices. A little after eight hours from boarding the bus he was in New York.

From there he planned to travel South West into West Virginia, then due west across the top of Kentucky, the bottom of Illinois and then on into Missouri and Kansas. Somewhere in the wilds of Missouri or Kansas he hoped to lose himself for a while. Whether this would also prove so easy; to find a place to stay, to find casual work without the requisite Green Card he had no idea. Someone would probably give him work, on a pittance because they knew he could hardly complain. Those were the cards he'd been dealt, or so he figured and he planned to make the best of it.

Fate had other, better ideas. As if it was balancing the books for getting him into this mess in the first place. As the bus rolled out of New York he pondered the turn of events and wondered if he was actually making decisions for himself at all, or simply riding the conveyor belt.

CHAPTER FIVE - A NEW LIFE

He spent about forty hours on the bus, which brought home to him the enormity of the States, since by now he was in Kansas, not the west coast. Of course there had been rest breaks, but even so. He left the bus at a small town called Lindsborg. He'd chosen it as a place to stop and explore the possibility of carving out a new life, partly at random, but a number of things appealed to him. Its Swedish heritage appealed, he appreciated the fact that Swedes in Sweden identified with the British sense of humour and understood Monty Python in a way Americans generally didn't.

He'd also been to Sweden a few times and figured that since the Vikings had raped and pillaged so much of eastern Britain that our genes must be pretty similar, not to mention the fact that the Normans were just Norsemen who'd come via Italy and France. Yes, he liked the Scandinavian peoples, although these Swedes had been in the USA for generations and he guessed it was really a rather foolish romantic notion.

Then there was the size of the place, with a population around three thousand he'd read. It was hard to visualise a town of three thousand people unless you'd lived in such a place before, which he hadn't. Did it mean everyone knew everyone else and their business? That would be a negative, maybe it would be easier to get lost in a big city teeming with people who mostly ignore one another. Nonetheless he decided to give it a try; in such a place talking to people might lead to casual work more easily than in somewhere like Chicago or LA and he felt he'd simply feel more at home in a small place so long as his presence there didn't elicit too much interest.

These thoughts didn't really constitute a high degree of planning mind you, but he couldn't stay on the bus forever and after alighting at Lindsborg he wandered Main Street before settling in a bar called Farleys, which was also a grill and ordering a burger and a beer, money was low enough now not to consider a steak.

His waitress introduced herself as Sarah and he took in her short skirt with bibbed front, white blouse and braces crossed behind. She had tall shoes but with sturdy heels, shapely legs, trim waist, shoulder length dark brown hair, enough make up, but not too much, nice lips and some blue eyeliner. He guessed she was early to mid thirties with a lovely smile but doleful doe like eyes that suggested to him that under the happy go lucky facade there lay a not entirely happy lady.

He wondered at himself assessing her so in his own current predicament and realised he'd been gazing into those sad, soulful eyes longer than was polite. He apologised and excused himself saying he'd been miles away. She smiled at his concern and his accent. She'd served an English family once before, their car had broken down and they were away as soon as possible, Brits were a rarity and Sarah liked the idea of talking to someone whose experiences and knowledge of the world were different from her own.

More than that, although she had nothing against the local guys, they had become boring and predictable. She wanted a sexual relationship, sure, but judging from the experiences of some of her friends, all the locals wanted was a quick shag and then off. That at least that was her opinion and she hadn't given anyone the opportunity, so had not technically confirmed it in the five years since her husband Billy, Billy the kid as she called him because he'd never grown up, had disappeared.

She'd been used to getting along without him anyhow, because he'd been in the army and even when he wasn't posted away he'd preferred drinking with the lads rather than spending time with her. Then came the motorcycle accident; he always rode too fast and took too many risks on the public highway, she'd long since declined to ride behind him. Coming out of a right hand bend too fast he'd found a car coming the other way, taking the apex or just maybe across it which the authorities couldn't determine, anyhow, it had ripped Billy's left leg off and he was lucky, they said, to have survived. Billy did not feel lucky.

Out of the army and not having been offered a desk job, for which he was temperamentally unsuited, he got some insurance money and an army pension that was paid into their joint account. He'd lost his leg midway down his shattered thigh and although prosthetics were tried it was all too difficult for a man sinking into drink and depression and he'd become glued to his wheelchair.

The trailer where they lived, out Assaria way, was modified but Billy spent most of his time in town anyway. Sarah had banned him from Farleys though; she needed the sanity of the job and Billy was drinking most of what went into the joint account.

She surreptitiously opened an account of her own at another bank. Billy was too far gone to notice and besides she needed to buy food for the both of them and pay for the pitch, she didn't see it as a deception.

Then one morning Billy didn't come home from his drinking in town, he didn't come home the next morning either. He'd become abusive and had tried to be violent on occasion, although it usually resulted in his falling out of the chair rather than any real physical damage to Sarah. Still, it was no way to live, his going away for a bit to cool off was a good thing.

After a week she wondered if she should report him missing, maybe he'd rolled into a ditch and died of exposure. She still couldn't bear to go to the sheriff's office. If a body turned up they'd tell her and for now she could say she understood he'd gone to stay with Maggie, his sister in Oklahoma. Everyone knew and liked Sarah, the idea that she'd lie about something like that wouldn't occur to them.

After two weeks it occurred to her to check their joint account, his pension had gone in and had not been touched. She withdrew some cash, bought flower tubs to set outside the trailer and some paint to spruce up the outside, she'd already made the inside spotless now there were no empty beer bottles and constant spillages.

After a month she thought she really ought to report him missing, but now the question would be why had she not done so before? Then there was the question of the pension, if he was declared dead it would stop, worse she might have to pay back money she'd already spent.

She told Angie at work that Billy had left her. Angie's husband had run off with a schoolmistress a couple of years ago saying Angie wasn't smart enough for him. Angie understood husbands leaving and she hadn't been bothered either. Angie, however, hadn't grown tired of local guys and enjoyed a healthy, as she saw it, and varied sex life, she enjoyed it and she figured if they were using her, well then she was using them right back.

Lived in the present did Angie, no thought for the future and she liked to talk, talk, talk, talk, so Sarah swore her to secrecy and knew that within twenty four hours everyone would know that Billy had left her, but that it was a secret and they mustn't say anything to Sarah. Sympathetic eyes told her the strategy had worked, but no one harangued her about it, which was all she asked, even the Sheriff assumed the story to be true and also assumed that Sarah knew where Billy had gone so no enquiries had been made.

That was five years ago and Sarah, a very different animal from Angie, hadn't had a man in the trailer since. She'd been out with guys a few times, but as soon as they showed any interest in something more Sarah stopped it dead in its tracks, not even a kiss. Kinder not to lead them on if she wasn't interested, and so she even stopped dating, earning herself a reputation for standoffishness and frigidity which was entirely unjustified, it was just that no one really knew her true nature, or even cared to try hard enough to find out.

She was just that pretty but prudish waitress with a smile for everyone and nothing going on. She was, in fact, interested in many things, love, life, sex, men, new experiences; her fantasies were rich and varied, she just wasn't interested in the people around her and she felt her life was being wasted, passing by in the same old dull routine despite the new comforts and freedoms at home. She just didn't have confidence enough to do something more about it.

She topped up Mike's coffee repeatedly and wondered at him sitting there for so long, she smiled as he visited the mens' room again and then again, but still kept drinking the coffee she offered him. It was a pretty quiet afternoon that went into a pretty quiet evening. Farley liked her to be friendly with the customers and not to rush them, offer them something more, which meant extra fries, not herself, but she could engage in conversation without incurring the wrath of the boss and she loved the sound of Mike's voice.

She too noticed something sad in his eyes whilst appreciating his manners, demeanour and warm kindly face. He wasn't flabby either she thought, 'nice guy wonder what he's doing here?' and so she started to ask him where he was from and how come he'd ended in Lindsborg, little knowing that Mike had been rehearsing a story for the last forty hours that he now put into effect.

He didn't want to appear depressed or a victim by nature, he wanted a place to stay and casual employment, so he talked about an urge to see the world, to experience new things, meet new people. Told her why he'd picked Lindsborg although not yet the bit about seeking anonymity. She asked him how long he intended to stay. He said he didn't know, it depended on finding a cheap place to stay and maybe some casual employment. The conversation had an unfortunate turn of events from Sarah's point of view as it focussed Mike's mind on the fact that he had nowhere to sleep and time was getting on.

He pointed this out to Sarah and said that in view of the time he really ought to be going to sort out a place to lay his head and could she recommend a cheap motel or something. Panicked at the thought he'd be gone as suddenly as he arrived, and knowing that another opportunity to meet someone fresh, new, attractive, intelligent, polite, grown up but not boring, with perfect manners who inspired confidence and many other justifications that rushed through her mind at breakneck speed she heard herself say "why don't you stay at mine, just until you know what you want to do."

In view of his dwindling dollars the suggestion appealed greatly and so, frankly, did Sarah, "well if you're happy for me to sleep on the couch, that would be wonderful he said".

"There's an old Landcruiser out back, I'm usually out within half an hour of closing if you hang around out there I'll take you home, I'm in Assaria, it's not far. "And since you're staying what about something else to eat to soak up all that coffee and keep my boss happy that I've sold you something?"

Figuring he'd saved a night's accommodation Mike ordered a club sandwich and settled down to watch the ice hockey until closing time. When he left at closing time he went out back and kept in the shadows until Sarah appeared, making it look like he'd just been taking a leak. No one ever paid Sarah any attention these days and no one saw her taking a strange man home, the idea would never have entered anyone's head anyway, everyone knew Sarah wasn't interested in guys.

At the trailer the first thing Mike noticed was the absence of a couch. He made mention of the fact and Sarah, more confident and natural now she was on her home turf smiled broadly and simply stated "you mentioned a couch, I didn't".

She explained that tomorrow was her day off and so there was no need to go straight to bed they could stay up and talk, and if he felt comfortable he could share her bed, but if not she'd clear a space on the floor. So they sat at the table and talked. She told him about Billy, she didn't know why she did it, didn't know why she trusted him, but all her instincts told her he would keep her secret and she'd yearned to unburden herself for oh so long now, it seemed an eternity.

She told him it all, life before the accident, life after, the drinking, the violence, her frustrations, the failings, as she saw them, of the local guys who were OK really but she didn't want to be passed around like Angie. It was growing light when fatigue finally overcame Sarah, just as Mike was trying to find a verbal, credible justification for his desire to keep a low profile. She took on board that he wanted or needed his privacy but little else as she undressed him and then herself and smiling led him to bed where she promptly fell asleep with her head on his chest and where ten minutes later, despite a whirlpool of thoughts he couldn't turn off and despite a slight feeling of arousal, fatigue physically defeated him too.

It was early afternoon when they stirred again Sarah made coffee and brought two steaming mugs back to bed, where Mike had just sat up. "At least I know how you take your coffee, cream no sugar".

"Thanks, can I freshen up?"

"Sure, through there."

It didn't take him long to quickly hose himself down with the shower head, he grabbed his toothbrush from his bag and freshened his mouth too. He felt slightly self conscious walking back naked, he saw that she had slipped on a kind of silken housecoat or dressing gown and had both removed her make up and brushed her hair. She was sitting on top of the covers on her side of the bed, her legs stretched out in front of her. He noticed how pretty her feet were and the silk slid off one leg, she didn't replace it just looked at him, both of them aware that something was stirring between his legs.

She stood up and kissed him allowing the silk robe to fall from her shoulders and puddle on the floor at her feet. She stood on tip toe and he felt her breasts against his chest. He was aware of her fingernails sliding down from his shoulder and gave an involuntary sigh as they pressed his nipple and a positive moan when she grasped his cock squeezed it and led him back to the bed by it.

They made love on and off for several hours, always respectfully, each thinking about giving pleasure to the other more than taking it. Although she had initiated it Sarah felt it was the best sex she'd had in her life, she felt he was the teacher, but she was a willing learner and without any inhibitions. She wondered if she was in love but didn't want to scare him away.

In the comfortable, warm afterglow experienced by two people who wanted the same things and still do, with no regrets or guilt, no misgivings, that natural harmony that can, but doesn't always follow lovemaking, they started to talk again.

Since she had done most of the talking the night before she wanted to know about him now. He told her he'd been a London taxi driver, liked to dance to swing music and had gone to clubs in London and twice to a dance camp in Sweden. It was interesting, it built a picture in so far as it went. She wanted to know about other women, but was afraid at what she might learn so she didn't probe too deeply. She kept coming back to why he'd left home and he tried to head her off by asking questions about Billy.

He wanted to tell her the truth, but thought it was rather too early; by their actions ye shall know them he thought and decided he'd inspire confidence by being a true English gent and by being good to her. He promised to tell all at a later date if they stayed together, but intimated that something painful and difficult had happened at home and that all he wanted was peace and not to be found, he intended to keep a low profile.

Whilst her curiosity was well and truly piqued Sarah was not unintelligent, she knew better than to push, because she knew exactly what she wanted and Mike O'Brien, Dave Harrison to her at this juncture, just might well be the answer to her prayers. A man she fancied to hell and back, who was satisfying in bed, to say the least of it, and who potentially would keep a lid on her situation whilst still staying around. How long for she had no idea, but she would make the most of every minute.

Knowing that many a true word is spoken in jest she asked him how he felt about being a kept man. "Right now, if it's you doing the keeping I'd think I was in heaven" he said, but added that he would do things for her, whatever needed doing to the trailer, or the truck and if there was a chance to earn some money discreetly he'd take it. And so it was that life settled into a new and delightful routine, money was no issue and for a while at least no one even noticed that Sarah had a man living with her. Although that wouldn't last, for the moment at least Mike O'Brien simply ceased to exist whilst enjoying a most delightful existence.

Of course people do notice things. At the grocery store old Mr Williams noticed that Sarah was buying more than usual, "Billy returned to the nest?" he inquired good naturedly.

"No she said and I'm not eating for two either!"

She wondered why she'd added that last bit since no one would think that of her and it did sort of imply there might be a man around. She decided in future to buy her normal amount shopping from old Mr Williams and top up at the Supermarket on the outskirts of Lindsborg where the conversation would stretch to 'have a nice day' and end there.

Mike mostly stayed in the trailer during the day and they took long walks together in the evening. For the first few weeks they spent most of her one day off a week in bed together. Mike had achieved many of his aims and escaped the likely loneliness into the bargain, but Sarah worked long hours and keeping the place clean, doing some laundry, making breakfast and dinner for both of them and his own lunch really didn't take up that much time.

He even hesitated to put the TV on as the sound carried but occasionally succumbed and put it on very low. He was of course especially interested in the news, but nothing appeared that had any relevance to his situation. He asked Sarah to buy him some books which she was only too happy to do for him, she worried about his hermit like way of going on, even though it suited her perfectly. He started with War And Peace, it took up plenty of time and immersed him in a new historical period and culture, but even that was read cover to cover in under a fortnight.

When he reached the point where Pierre, captured by the French, comes to the conclusion that his life is a concatenation of circumstances, that he is not controlling it, nor any one being or event Mike had felt a certain familial sympathy with the sentiment. He would put it in more modern terms, but he understood. From there he pondered that in his day and age such a thing was rare if not unique, but that throughout history men and women must have experienced this feeling in their millions.

Ancient towns had been sacked by Mesopotamians, Egyptians, Greeks, Romans, Goths, Visigoths, Mongols, Franks, Vikings, Normans, Bourbons, Turks, Napoleon through to the world wars. It was only post 1945 he surmised that people in Western Europe and Russia certainly had not known what it was to have their lives overturned by events outside their control. Whilst in other parts of the world, the Balkans, the Middle East, parts of Africa it was, even now continuing.

He may be unique in his own society, but certainly not in an historical or worldwide perspective. He didn't know it but Mike was changing, his philosophising seemed nothing more than daydreaming at the time, but if man is guided by his predominant thoughts, so Mike was setting himself up to become involved in world affairs, Not yet, but his dominating thoughts now would one day guide his actions.

When he wasn't reading or in one of these reveries Mike tried to think of everything he could do to make life better for Sarah and so it wasn't long before his presence was noted, one of the neighbours spotted him watering the plants and started to gossip. The owner of the trailer park knocked on the door during the day when he knew Sarah would be at work and feigned surprise, said he'd heard the TV and assumed Sarah was home. Mike had ascertained the volume at which the TV could not be heard outside, but said nothing other than that he'd tell Sarah she was wanted at the office and closed the door.

That night Mike and Sarah discussed a common hymn sheet. They decided that the two of them had met years ago as teenagers when Mike had had a ski holiday in Wyoming and so had she. No one really knew anything about Sarah's early life so that was credible. They'd stayed in touch, just birthdays and Christmas and then when Mike's long term partner had left him and after a period of depression he'd written to Sarah and well, one thing had led to another and he'd come out to see her, but you know what these Englishmen are like, very private people, not like us.

Having faced up to the problem, life became easier again, Mike could go out talk to people, he too became part of the scenery, Sarah introduced him to people, he became accepted. Even the Sheriff who saw Sarah had lost that defeated look in her eyes wanted to help.

"I'll not be enquiring about Green Cards or anything of the sort if the boy finds work" he said. "It's good to see you happy Sarah, god knows if anyone deserves it it's you".

Mike found himself fixing a car here, doing some painting and decorating there. He earned a reputation for politeness, reliability, punctuality and for not bullshitting, if he didn't feel qualified for a job he'd say so and turn it down, if he could do it he'd do it and do it well. People liked that.

He was even getting used to the name Dave, but wondered when and if he should tell Sarah, at least, his real circumstances.

CHAPTER SIX - A QUESTION OF DIPLOMACY

A report landed on the desk of George J. Tenet, Director of CIA. He didn't take kindly to his highly trained and expensively equipped agents making basic mistakes and losing people they were supposed to have under close scrutiny. He had no great love for the Brits, but was closely acquainted with Sir Richard Dearlove the head of MI6 in London, who had at one time been the head of Washington Station for MI6 in the USA.

Of course it hadn't been MI6 who'd lost the laptop, but MI5 and that was the responsibility of Sir Stephen Lander, who like Dearlove was an alumni of Queens College Cambridge. Whatever the two heads of the SIS, Special Intelligence Services the umbrella term for MI5 and 6 thought of one another they wouldn't let the old boy network down, they'd stick together.

MI6 dealt with international intelligence work and MI5 with things at home in the UK. For such close allies as the UK and USA, with a so called special relationship, there was a considerable degree of mistrust and a mutual lack of respect as regards the leaky nature of first one side and then the other, which is why the CIA had been trailing an MI5 man in the first place. In fact in security circles the special relationship frankly did not exist at all.

Politically this relationship waxed and waned but with Blair and Clinton rubbing along like old chums at that point everything would have to be put on the table. Tenet's first call was to Dearlove his second to the President. Dearlove appraised Lander and the pair arranged an urgent meeting with the Prime Minister. Both parties knew that there had been failings on both sides, only Dearlove as yet still smelled more or less of roses.

Lander arranged for the interrogation of James Lancaster who had only that morning confessed what had happened. He'd told the whole truth, everything, including how Suzy Lancaster had inadvertently shouted out information that could lead someone to hit upon his password, not that she knew what passwords he used. He'd been ashamed, disgusted with himself, genuinely remorseful and was of course under lock and key. His wife was under surveillance, his career ruined yet those at the head of MI5 were convinced that he'd been overworked and careless but was absolutely not a traitor. The American side were just as convinced that he was in fact the loose cannon they were looking for.

Tony Blair and Bill Clinton didn't want to prompt media speculation by meeting ahead of their next scheduled tête a tête which was some two months away but discussed options for some three hours via the scrambled hotline.

It was decided that Dearlove and Tenet would work together on the security issue and that UK and US scientists would independently develop, improve and miniaturise the technology, at the same time as increasing its range and control functions. They would later share their findings with a view to both nations sharing the weapon whose greatest value lay in its secrecy, that secrecy which had been compromised within weeks of the initial discovery, due to blunders by both UK intelligence services and US intelligence services. More heads would roll than Lancaster's alone.

In order not to arouse interest in the ranks Dearlove and Tenet selected one man each to work together. They were to have anything and almost everything they needed whenever they wanted it via a simple request to the two intelligence chiefs, but, what they would not have was a big team working full time for them, as that would involve far too much explanation, potential for another leak and frankly too much embarrassment.

CIA operative Kevin Donohue was despatched after a two hour briefing to London to meet Sean Hobbs of MI6. The two men chosen were regarded by their respective bosses as the best they had, not too young, not too impulsive. They were also chosen because it was thought they would work well together which involved a few assumptions.

Donohue, was a former Green Beret thirty eight years of age, he was a university graduate, raised in the Bronx who'd made it to Johns Hopkins University in Maryland on the back of talent, ambition and downright determination. He'd rapidly transferred from the 101st Airborne to the Green Berets and was coming up for ten years served in the intelligence services. He spoke three languages fluently, but although you can take the boy out of the Bronx, you can't ever take the Bronx out of the boy, or the man come to that. Accents were about his most obvious weakness and less obvious a tendency to rush to conclusions and to never doubt or question his own judgement for a second.

Hobbs had been raised in Surrey, the son of a competent police inspector and the detective work side of things had rubbed off in long chats with his father as he grew up. Not public school, but quite old school in his way of conducting himself, Donohue would find him an enigma. From the Royal Marines Hobbs had progressed to the SBS, that's the Special Boats Service, Britain's maritime equivalent of the SAS or Special Air Service. Like Donohue he'd kept himself in shape but at forty two was a little over four years older. He was slower to act and more thoughtful than Donohue who like to pitch right in.

Hobbs's desire to spend more time on cerebral activities rather than rushing about chasing the first idea that came into his head, combined with his home counties accent, which would not have sounded at all up itself to any Brit, especially compared with almost any old Etonion, Harrow or Tonbridge boy nonetheless got Donohue's goat and reinforced his prejudices.

Their military backgrounds were supposed to make them a compatible team in the minds of their bosses, but inter services rivalry is not unusual, the Marines and the Paras don't always see eye to eye in the UK for example and Donohue was out of the US equivalent stable in Hobbs's eyes. Throw in a degree of national rivalry and mistrust, the cultural and attitudinal differences and with both nations at fault in this particular cock up things didn't get off to a good, or an especially speedy start.

After his briefing Hobbs went to Heathrow to meet Donohue, who was all for jumping in the car and heading straight to Cambridgeshire without so much as a how do you do and let's discuss what's happened, compare ideas and formulate a plan. Hobbs insisted on slowing things down as Donohue saw it. Hobbs felt that by comparing ideas discussing things in detail and formulating a plan of action the efficiency saving would make things quicker in the long run. Donohue felt they could do all their talking in the car. Hobbs, who was the sole driver at this juncture, thought otherwise.

Tenet and Dearlove had impressed on both men the need for a harmonious relationship and both were aware of the personal interest being taken by President and Prime Minister, both were aware of the problems which could arise from the technology falling into the wrong hands, but both men had assumed the other would see things through the same lens as themselves and that clearly was not going to be the case. Falling out over it was not an option, both men would bend a little to make the partnership work, but not easily. Oh no, not easily.

CHAPTER SEVEN - OLD FASHIONED POLICE WORK

In the first instance Hobbs won out, mostly because he was on home turf and had the car. A separate car was available for Donohue, but it awaited him in London. Hobbs took Donohue home to his town house in Islington, his wife was visiting her mother in Scotland, Donohue could have the guest room and they could talk things through and, just as his dad would have done, think things through. As far as Hobbs was concerned old fashioned police work was what was needed initially.

He wasn't convinced that O'Brien was a spy, far from it, primarily because he had been involved in debriefing and questioning Lancaster who he was convinced had screwed up, but wasn't working for any outside party. If that conclusion was correct, and he felt pretty confident about it, that would make the taxi driver an innocent in the wrong place at the wrong time. An unduly nosey innocent, but still, not a spy.

Donohue was far from convinced about Lancaster, after all, his own colleagues had been tailing Lancaster and he knew the basis of their suspicions, but he wasn't able to share that information with Hobbs, as that would only open up another can of worms about leaks relating to another matter.

Nonetheless, he had to agree with Hobbs that since Lancaster was already in custody and that the real threat was the knowledge in O'Brien's head, catching O'Brien as swiftly as possible was the key to everything. Given the British laptop had been in US custody and copied prior to return to the Brits, both nations now had a vested interest in keeping the knowledge to themselves.

Debriefing the CIA guys at the house in Cambridgeshire was important, but a plan for how to track down O'Brien was more important. The CIA team, in disgrace, had been ordered to leave O'Brien's house alone, the local police had been instructed to seal it and to keep a man on duty to prevent anyone else entering, but without the sort of show that would make local people and especially the media suspicious.

A woman called Rachel had called at the Romford address and had been told that Mr O'Brien was missing after a break in and had further been told that they had a lead which would be compromised if the media got involved, so would she please be very discreet and someone would be round to interview her if she'd be so kind as to leave her details, which she had done.

This was a stroke of luck for O'Brien since Rachel knew nothing and could only be a waste of precious time for the security services. Donohue would be all for interrogating her his way. Hobbs wanted to take the gentle approach and here in the UK he insisted it was his call. He also pointed out that Donohue's accent would be a distraction at best and something that would need explaining at worst. Donohue dismissed the notion that he couldn't pass for British if he needed to.

It was agreed they'd go to the safe house first, see how O'Brien had escaped, view the interrogation videos personally and then pay a visit to Rachel before meeting forensics in Romford. After settling on a course of action for the first full day of working together Hobbs took Donohue to dinner and tried to build some kind of bond. Having been working on something else just a few short hours earlier Hobbs thought his experience was a bit like the experience the salmon on his plate had suffered trying to get upstream before being rudely yanked from the water, no pun on yanked intended but working with Donohue would, he thought, test his patience.

The next morning Hobbs was up at six am to prepare breakfast and found a note from Donohue to say he'd already gone for a run but would be back at six thirty. Hobbs made a traditional British breakfast, which wasn't the healthy option Donohue announced he'd have preferred, nonetheless he tucked in heartily. By seven thirty they were on their way to the safe house where all those involved in the capture and loss of O'Brien might be interviewed.

Statements had already been scrutinised by both Hobbs and Donohue and questions prepared. Further, the several days of video had been edited down to two hours of highlights, there simply wasn't time or necessity for the investigating team to sit through the hours of inactivity, although complete copies of every tape were given to both men in case they wished to look through them later.

The morning was embarrassing for Donohue, but Hobbs took no advantage and kept everything as straightforward and professional as possible. An appointment had been made to interview Rachel, but since she worked this had only been possible after six pm and so their next stop was to the house in Romford where they met the forensics team.

Forensics had been there previously of course and were finishing up. Photographs had been taken and everything had been dusted for fingerprints. Samples of hair, skin particles and household dust had been taken, the whole nine yards in fact, but forensic evidence would help very little if at all in this case.

It was already known who O'Brien had seen, who had passed him the laptop, who his girlfriend was, who had abducted him and who had lost him. All forensics would confirm once a swab had been requested and given was that Rachel had been there, probably frequently, she and O'Brien were intimate and that she kept some toiletries and a toothbrush in the house. All of which she was happy to tell them in any case.

She would also be able to confirm that certain items of clothing were missing, but not many and the investigating team knew that anyway since it was the CIA who'd taken them. It confirmed O'Brien had not been back, but that was a given too, had he returned he'd be in custody again and none of this would be necessary.

The fact that a man with just the clothes he stood up in, no money in his pocket, no passport could disappear completely in the twinkling of an eye indicated outside help certainly. Donohue put this down to near conclusive proof that he was working for a rival intelligence agency. Hobbs simply deduced that someone was sheltering or assisting him. Neither dreamed he'd be out of the country before they'd even teamed up. In fact it had been a close run thing at Heathrow, had they but known, O'Brien left scant hours before Donohue arrived.

Forensics had taken O'Brien's ageing desktop computer with its early version of Windows and would provide Donohue and Hobbs with copies of every file and photograph on it which they could study alongside his videos at their leisure. Clearly there was a lot of homework to do and little time in which to do it if they were to satisfy their respective masters.

They were torn between asking for help in this analysis and the need to give anyone else involved some information as to what they were looking for and why. Since increasing the size of the team was at this point not acceptable to those above them in the chain of command, they could only ask straightforward questions of others on the periphery and to be certain they'd have to look through absolutely everything themselves.

With his detective's instincts Hobbs relished this side of things even though it was long and laborious. Donohue hated it and chafed for action, but did what was necessary. They decided to look at everything independently the next day at Hobbs's house but in separate rooms and in this way a competitive element crept in, who would spot something vital the other missed, and so that at least motivated Donohue.

The most important clue they left Romford with was O'Brien's address book. They also took his diary, box files of bills and other papers, but the address book was the key. However, the following day would be spent building up a picture of O'Brien, his parents, his education, his work record and where he'd been on holidays.

During the time they spent building up this picture of their man, O'Brien would be moving on, he'd be swiftly forgotten by the hotel staff in Montreal and the taxi driver. He would also be long forgotten by the people on and the drivers of the Greyhound buses he'd used, by the time Donohue and Hobbs were ready to pursue him.

He was just a face in the crowd and he'd destroyed the credit cards that might give him away, he really had disappeared most effectively whilst Donohue and Hobbs were just getting into doing their background work.

After leaving the house in Romford they went to see O'Brien's hair stylist, the lovely Rachel who he'd fallen for the first time she cut his hair and leaned into his head with her soft warm bosom, a ploy she used with most men who visited the salon to help guarantee repeat business.

Rachel was at home as expected for this appointment, in her one bedroom flat above the salon. A real Essex girl, Rachel's taste in décor was not the same as either Hobbs's or even Donohue's. Her personality wouldn't appeal to Hobbs particularly, but her personal, more physical attractions were undeniable, fit, sexy, nice hands and feet, polished nails and of course nice hair, a bit too much face powder but provocative in her own way. Donohue thought he'd go there under different circumstances, or that maybe, if the opportunity arrived he should pump her for information. Not a thought he'd share with Hobbs.

As soon as they walked in Rachel observed "you're a couple of fit specimens for Romford coppers aren't you" it was a statement not a question, but Hobbs felt an answer was required.

"We take kidnapping very seriously Miss and a life could be in danger so we've been drafted in. Besides which, the boys at Romford have a lot to do policing the centre, Thursday through Saturday nights especially; lively place isn't it, quite a lot of drinking on the streets, that sort of thing, it's a question of resources."

"Sure, anyway what can I help you chaps with? Oh sorry do you want a cuppa?"

"No thanks."

"Coffee would be nice Miss." Said Donohue in his best British accent.

"You're a long way from home aren't you, that's the Big Apple, Bronx I'm guessing?"

There was no point making things worse. "Exchange posting, one of yours is doing my job at home, learning experience."

"I expect he'll learn more in the Bronx than you will in Romford, how do you take it?"

"Cream no sugar please."

"It's instant and semi skimmed milk I'm afraid, back in a mo."

Donohue and Hobbs sat in high backed chairs at the table. After handing Donohue his coffee, Rachel in miniskirt and heels took the opportunity of a Sharon Stone moment sinking into the settee and crossing her legs suggestively.

The interview with Rachel was uninformative other than to help paint a picture of O'Brien as a bit of a lad who liked the women, but treated them with respect. Rachel playfully informed them she'd had to teach him a thing or two.

Over dinner in a local Tandoori Donohue expressed the view that he wasn't taken in one bit and that surveillance of Rachel would have to continue. Hobbs agreed, verbally at least, he wasn't footing the bill and no point contradicting his partner over anything so unimportant, it would make it easier to get his way when it really mattered. Give in on the little things, dig in on the big issues.

An office had been set aside for Donohue and Hobbs at SIS on the Embankment and they took adjoining rooms in the Park Plaza Hotel while they worked together in London. Only they had access to their workroom, not even coffee breaks were taken outside, no one else in or out, except Dearlove, and Tenet in the unlikely event he paid them a visit, that would certainly pique curiosity in the building however and wasn't on the cards.

On day two, Hobbs, doing things the old way, started pinning paper, notes, names and pictures to the wall with known movements etcetera. It didn't amount to a lot. Hard drives were delivered, one for each of them, each with the contents of O'Brien's desktop PC. In common with the interview Rachel had given everything pointed to a man who enjoyed life's pleasures, was reasonably intelligent, not particularly ambitious although he worked hard and liked money. A substantial amount of cash had been found in a locked gun cabinet in the loft but they weren't interested in tax evasion. Most cash businesses swindled a bit.

Hobbs came more and more to believe he was getting a handle on who O'Brien was, Donohue saw an elaborate smoke screen, a cleverly concealed sleeper working for a foreign power, probably Russia, but could be Iran, China, even North Korea, or any other perceived enemy of Uncle Sam. He didn't believe a taxi driver could squirrel away so much cash either, that was for his nefarious spy work and had been provided by his controllers, obviously, how could Hobbs not see that?

CHAPTER EIGHT – THE FIRST BREAKTHROUGH

Things went badly for Donohue and Hobbs from the outset, mostly because they both felt rushed, even the fast moving, impulsive Donohue felt pressured for a quick result and Hobbs felt himself to be under even more pressure to go quickly from both his bosses and now his new unwanted partner. The old adage more haste less speed was never more true.

O'Brien's address book and email account threw up over four hundred family and friends in contacts, and then there were all the girls he'd met dancing and on dating sites. He'd dallied with another fifty or so of those, all of whom would need to be interviewed too. There was no way Donohue and Hobbs were going to conduct close to four hundred and fifty interviews personally and so they called upon the resources available to them and had others do the leg work while they studied papers and computer files.

Every contact, friend and relative of O'Briens would be questioned concerning his disappearance from the point of view of trying to track a man they were worried for, someone who might have been kidnapped. Ordinary everyday coppers could do that without raising suspicion, Donohue and Hobbs would pen the questions, but they wouldn't get to look into the person's eyes, detect the lie or probe anything that might sound strange to them.

Of course what they should have done was to prioritise, by studying email and phone records it would have been easy to understand who was closest to O'Brien and to do those interviews themselves, but this opportunity they passed up, primarily as a result of too much speed, although the fact that the person closest to their quarry had not helped one iota may have contributed to the making of this basic error. They were still working out who was who and trying to piece together a history of O'Brien's movements and social diary, concurrent with the delegated interviews taking place.

At these remote interviews everyone answered the questions openly and honestly, with one exception and although Donohue and Hobbs had saved time by not travelling to see all these people personally they still needed to listen to all the recordings. Weeks passed unproductively.

During those weeks Rachel had not been herself. Sexually active party animal that she was, she hadn't been unfaithful to Mike yet, she saw him as missing not dead and felt that he'd contact her if he could. In which she was partially right, he could physically have phoned or written, but not without giving himself away and so in fact he could not. Her social life she had curtailed for now.

Rachel had been thinking about trying to get together with Mike's friend Dave down in Tunbridge Wells, she'd always fancied him, but that would have been taking the guilt of infidelity a stage further, him being Mike's best friend and all, and so she'd refrained from even calling him. The temptation was growing though and with her phone tapped and herself under surveillance she could easily have inadvertently increased Donohue and Hobbs's interest in the only person useful to them, but all temptation to alleviate her frustrations with Dave Harrison were alleviated when the fit American policeman paid her a visit.

"Oh it's you, come in. More questions?"

"No not really, it's more that I fancied some attractive female company and I haven't met many girls here yet, I'll go if it's a problem of course, but I wondered if you'd like to go for a drink?"

It wasn't difficult to seduce her she appreciated his hard muscled body, the curiosity aroused by someone foreign and different caused another kind of arousal too and so it was that Rachel's affair with Donohue rather than providing insight closed off a lead that would in all probability have come about somewhat sooner than it actually did.

Even Rachel knew she wouldn't wait for Mike forever and Dave Harrison had been her number one target. She would have lead them in the right direction, not now she had a new distraction though. Of course in regular police work getting involved with a witness was a punishable offence, in his line of work Donohue could justify it as a necessary self sacrifice to get closer to the subject, pillow talk often paid off.

Rachel hadn't thought to wonder about the rights or wrongs of a policeman getting involved with her. She quizzed Donohue about Mike as much as he probed her. He told her that the case was still active and that he shouldn't really be seeing her, but given he'd be going back to New York at sometime in the not too distant future it was now or never.

He put forward the thought that he couldn't risk losing the opportunity of getting to know a lovely English rose, which naturally flattered Rachel, as it was intended to, and which despite a little suspicion she chose to believe. She might even have harboured dreams of life in the States, but she felt she was somehow batting out of her league and best just enjoy it while she could and so she did, to the full.

Donohue also tried to put her off the scent by saying that without new information there was no way of knowing where her ex was and that that being the case he didn't see why he should refrain from seeing her. He even led her to believe that although the case remained open he was working on something else. Nothing he said or did brought forth anything of value. No harm trying though he thought as he rolled her over onto her front, in which he was precisely wrong.

Six months later things were getting very difficult for Hobbs and Donohue, results were demanded and with no leads to follow the two men went back to what they should have done in the first instance and prioritised O'Brien's contacts and finally, finally they paid a visit to Tunbridge Wells.

Given the time that had passed Dave Harrison felt able to unburden himself and when Donohue and Hobbs identified themselves fully he really felt he had no choice, he'd do almost anything for Mike but he didn't want to do jail time and he knew he was already very close given he hadn't been honest with the copper who'd called six months ago. Holding out might work, but certainly not if they caught Mike.

"OK" he said, "Look I helped Mike get away, but he had been kidnapped and had escaped, he was terrified his life was in danger and I helped him. I didn't tell the copper who called round because Mike had said he didn't know who to trust and I didn't know what resources the kidnappers might have. If you're going to prosecute me for that I'll take a lawyer now, in fact I'll have a lawyer anyway thanks, but if you guarantee immunity I'll tell you everything I know. Your call."

Hobbs was on the phone immediately. "We've got him, or at least we will have, I need an interview room at Tunbridge Wells police station and a lawyer for the witness we'll be there in ten minutes."

"Can I have a word outside. What the fuck are you doing? He doesn't need a lawyer we'll get what we want and the hell with immunity from prosecution he's cost us six effing months."

"My jurisdiction, my call AND it'll be quicker this way, he'll talk openly and frankly this way and we don't need a public prosecution against someone accidentally caught up in this."

"Yeah, if it is an accident and he's not part of the organisation, he'll spin us a story alright, but if he's working for another intelligence service... Jeez you Limeys."

CHAPTER NINE – TANYA

It's debatable whether Phillips in Hamilton County, Nebraska should be termed a village or a hamlet, it's not far from Grand Island, which might be termed a small town, but still pretty much everyone knows everyone else's business in places like these. To say it's the back of beyond is possibly to put it kindly.

Although of average height and without the classical benefits of blonde hair and blue eyes Tanya Brown was fast becoming a living legend in Hamilton County and even beyond. At twenty two she was at the height of her beauty, the most incredible looker to come out of Nebraska most of the menfolk said. Everything about her was perfect, her complexion, her perfectly balanced figure, slim waist, shapely legs. She had bobbed brown hair, nothing out of the ordinary, except that it framed her soft features, large soulful brown eyes and bewitching lips in a way that drew you in, made people want to stare and dream. Even the local women and her old school friends acknowledged Tanya was one in a million, but she was so nice it was hard to be jealous. What's more the only person who didn't appreciate how incredibly beautiful she was, was Tanya herself. Possibly her most alluring feature.

She knew men looked at her in a certain way, but thought, perhaps correctly, that they look at all young women that way. She'd left school and gone to work at an auto showroom as receptionist. Her boyfriend was the son of the owner. Despite cajoling, exclamations of undying love, a ridiculous engagement ring and attempts at inebriating her he'd so far failed to get into her knickers, (pants in American vernacular) much to his frustration, and embarrassment. Had anyone known about this failure it would have been even worse; they did know, naturally everyone knew because everyone knew Tanya.

However, he fully expected everything would work out once they'd married. He felt proprietorial towards her, everyone was jealous that he had her and they didn't. He'd pluck her cherry even if he had to marry her to do it and then she'd be all his, the legend would be his alone.

The Browns had persuaded Tanya, much against her own instincts, not to go to university. Tanya wanted to see a city, experience new places, new people as well as learn something more. Her grades at high school had been exemplary and she applied herself, she knew she had a good brain and she wanted to use it. To grow as a person. Her mom wanted to hang on to Tanya forever, didn't want to lose her baby. Besides it's a dangerous world out there.

In the parochial world where she'd been raised however it was still largely considered unnecessary for girls to have a university education, more important for boys and anyway there was a job waiting for her at the Auto Store, she didn't need a higher education, she'd marry Jim Junior and be part of a successful family business. Life all mapped out, just not by her.

Jim Junior might have had the opportunity, as a boy child, to go to university, if he'd wanted to and if his grades had been good enough, but he'd been more interested in spending his parents' money even at school. He had no ambition to grow and expand his mind, who needed university when your dad was the most successful businessman around, you drove a Lexus, had the best looking girl and one day the business would be all yours too. Pa had two outlets now, his mom was receptionist at the one, his girl receptionist at the other. Jim Junior thought he had it all.

Jim's mom Brenda adored Tanya, she was a good girl, she'd keep her Jim Junior on the straight and narrow and there would be grandchildren, beautiful grandchildren. Jim Senior loved her because sales had more than doubled since she'd gone on reception and buyers seemed to be coming in from Kansas and all over. Tanya's parents assumed she'd marry Jim, her prom partner, Brenda and both the Jims also assumed it, and everyone wanted it and was looking forward to it. Except Tanya. Mrs Brown, Sandra, saw marriage to Jim Junior and a job at the Auto Store as a way of keeping her daughter close to home. Everyone knew what they wanted for Tanya.

When plans started being made without so much as a proposal from Jim Junior, or a by your leave from her parents, or his, it was the final straw.

CHAPTER TEN – DECISION TIME AGAIN

Mike O'Brien had started to feel lucky again. He'd long thought that the only two certainties in life were death and taxes and here he was, with a roof over his head, flimsy, but still a roof, food in his tummy, enjoyable work coming in from decent people, a lovely woman in bed with him every night and no taxes!

Back in the UK his best buddy had caved in and spilled all, but six months on the trail had gone pretty cold. Unbeknownst to O'Brien, Donohue and Hobbs were even now in the USA but still struggling. They'd found his flight to Montreal easily enough, found the hotel where he'd stayed, but no one there really remembered him, even from a photo. No one knew where he'd gone or how he'd travelled for sure. Dave Harrison had told them about a discussion where plans to take a Greyhound Bus and lose himself somewhere in the USA had been talked about but even he couldn't be sure Mike had done that. After all Canada is a nice place, no language difficulties and lots of small towns there too.

Asking the Canadians to look for O'Brien would necessitate explaining why and that was still unacceptable, the object was to minimise the number of people who knew about this thing not increase it. For now Donohue and Hobbs had to work on the theory that O'Brien had crossed the border. That should of course be documented but somehow there seemed to be a problem with record keeping and much fuss had been made about it, but no definite results yet.

Hobbs being keener on the detective side of things looked at the spiders web map of Greyhound routes and realised the enormity of the problem, not to mention that with so much time having elapsed that even if they found out where O'Brien left the bus that didn't mean he'd be anywhere near there now. The two of them could hardly investigate every back woods town that had a Greyhound stop.

A decision was taken to circulate O'Brien's out of date photo to every Sheriff's office as being a missing person from the UK who it was believed could possibly be in the USA. The problem was they didn't feel able to say national security issue, urgent, get on with it since that would be in the media within hours at most. There was little to do but wait.

Down in Lindsborg the Sheriff received a fax and thought it looked a bit like Sarah's fellow, even though his name was apparently Dave. He headed out to the trailer, but Mike was out on a job and no one knew who for, so the Sheriff went for a coffee and showed the fax to Sarah.

"There's no way that's Dave" she said with her most convincing laugh. She thought it was convincing anyway.

"Nonetheless I'll pop round when I've got a mo and ask him Sarah, I guess somewhere folks are worried about this guy gone missing."

"Sure thing Pop", Sarah's affectionate name for the Sheriff was Pop, no relation but she was as fond of him as he was of her. He'd follow through though, that much was certain, it was work and although it wasn't a priority there wasn't much to keep a Sheriff busy in Lindsborg. She thought about suggesting that Dave was a very private person and that even if it was him he must have reasons for not wanting his relatives to know where he was.

In fact it's normal that the authorities don't abuse the privacy of someone who wants to disappear from family and so on, their main interest is normally that the person is alive and safe, but then they'll want to know that person is living legally and whilst the local police had no idea why this Mike O'Brien was sought, they couldn't cover for an illegal alien, working illegally and not paying taxes, not once it was exposed, however much everyone liked the guy and found him useful, a contributing member of society in so many ways.

That evening Mike would have to make some swift choices, just as he'd had to more than half a year back. He immediately knew he had to do it, but he didn't feel at all happy about abandoning Sarah in much the same way as he'd abandoned Rachel, although at least he could give a partial explanation and say goodbye this time. He felt the loss of the new life he'd already come to enjoy keenly too.

Sarah was pure gold, how could he ever make it up to her? Mike had a fair amount of cash stashed, old habits die hard. Sarah had a ton of cash too, she'd always worried that the pension would come to an end and worse she'd have to pay money back. In order to have untraceable money she'd regularly withdrawn far more than she needed, but because she did it every month it looked like a lifestyle choice, no one imagined she had many thousands of dollars in a fireproof safe hidden behind a panel under the bed.

Mike confessed to Sarah that he'd discovered a terrible secret in something that had been left in the back of his taxi, he said that as a result of knowing more than he should he'd run away. He didn't tell her he'd been kidnapped and drugged, too much detail. He couldn't tell her what it was all about for her own safety he said, but swore he was on the side of the angels.

She didn't really need to be told that, she'd said, she already knew it, but she heard him out anyway. He hadn't gone to the authorities because, well, there were so many reasons, but would she just trust him? She knew him well enough to know he was one of the good guys didn't she?

It was enough for Sarah, the sadness which was palpable in him brought her to tears. It had been the happiest, seven months now, of her life, she wept for him and she wept for her own loss, but, no matter what, she wanted Mike, as she now knew him, safe and in the land of the living. Sarah, no stranger to tough decisions and hard knocks herself would do all in her power to keep her Mike free and alive even if they couldn't be together.

Sarah handed Mike the keys to the Toyota and said "you'd better take the pink slip too" handing him a battered piece of paper with Billy's name on it.

"What's this, it's not pink either!"

"It's, you know, it proves you own the vehicle, never changed it from Billy, good it's a blokes name eh, you can sell the old thing with this if it helps, they never were pink in Nebraska, just what they call them, they were pink once, in California or somewhere I think.

I want you to take this too, she handed him twenty five thousand dollars in used notes."

"Sarah I can't, I've got five thou that I've earned."

"Look I can't account for it and I've got the same amount again left over, so don't worry about me, get going tonight, when Pop comes round I'll tell him you've gone to buy lumber down south and you'll be back in a few days.

He'll wait a few days anyway so that'll buy you some time, but not much. I should go north just in case. Then when you don't reappear I'll have to say that maybe it was you in the fax after all and that you've abandoned me, I can say I gave you the truck ages ago so it's not reported stolen, he'll just feel sorry for me. I'll be fine, really."

She didn't look or sound fine, her voice was choked, her face red and blotchy, her eyes streaming.

Mike was paralysed at the sight of her, the guilt, the money, the vehicle, he was on the verge of just handing himself in, he started to make excuses for not getting going.

"How will you get to work?"

"I'll call Angie she'll get me there, when you don't come back I'll buy a new car, something I like!"

The more she put a brave face on things the more Mike couldn't stand it, he wept too, hugged her and shook, until finally she pushed him away and begged him to go and not to remember her like this.

She heard the truck start up and the scrunch of tyres then threw herself on the bed, their bed, buried her head in the pillow till it was sodden, then cried some more.

CHAPTER ELEVEN – A CHANCE ENCOUNTER

Following Sarah's advice Mike O'Brien decided to head vaguely north on the 81 then thought smaller roads might be slower but safer, be watched less and switched to the 14. A decision which would have profound consequences. Having left late evening, after a couple of hours or so, he pulled into a diner, grabbed a coffee, found it didn't have the desired effect and fell asleep in the cab of the old Toyota out in the car park.

Wakened by the sunrise, with the diner still closed he drove slowly on, not wanting to attract attention to himself by driving too quickly. After an hour he spotted a figure at the roadside thumbing a lift. Figuring, well, he wasn't quite sure what he was figuring at the time, but would later tell himself it was all logical, if anyone was looking for him they wouldn't be looking for a couple. That was actually a thought that came to him later, but the mind plays tricks.

In truth though he saw a beautiful girl and at the speed he was doing was able to recognise that fact. Maybe he figured she'd be safer with him than someone else, maybe he figured some company, any company, would do him good and maybe it was just the wow factor, although the girl was not dressed to kill. She was dressed to travel and walk if necessary. She had a small holdall and nothing more.

He pulled over, "where are you going?"

"Same place you're going."

"You don't know where I'm going."

"You leaving here?"

"Sure."

"Then I'm going where you're going."

"You better climb in then."

At which point her smile unmanned him completely and he didn't say anything just pulled back on the highway. They sat in silence for ten minutes then simultaneously.

"Where are you...."

"You first, is that a British accent?"

"Yep although I'm trying to lose it!"

"Why?"

"Long story, lets just say I'm running away from something, don't worry I'm not a criminal or anything, how about you."

"Oh, I'm running away too!"

They laughed, the ice well and truly broken. Tanya found him intriguing, she'd hardly met anyone from the wider world let alone abroad. For the first time in her life she discovered a coquettish side to herself, never before in her life had she flirted with anyone, let alone an older man, a man who would know things she only dreamed vaguely, innocently and ignorantly about to be blunt with herself.

There had never been a need to flirt with the local boys, they were all wandering clumsy hands without needing any encouragement anyway. They wouldn't know what flirting was and any hint of encouragement from her would lead to pressure. In a way that's why she'd dated Jim Junior; his parents wouldn't allow that kind of thing, a word from her and he'd be well grounded. Nonetheless, being known as Jim's girl and everyone knowing Jim's pa and their fathers' doing business with him pretty well provided her a degree of protection.

Her virginity, not to say lack of experience, was something she pondered frequently in her own mind, she wasn't going to lose it to some fumbling nobody who knew no more about it than she did, and who, would next morning, go straight out to brag about his conquest, she'd seen too many of her friends disillusioned and tearful from that scenario.

Part of her wanted to save herself for the man she would love and marry, another part of her just wanted to be wild and free, but also happy, not regretful. Tanya had been a late developer in some ways because she'd been so sheltered, her teenage angst and teenage insecurities and indecision had lingered on longer than normal. Her true self may never have burst forth at all were it not for the fury, no other word for it, she felt towards her family and Jim's for thinking they owned her to the extent they could plan her life without even asking a single question about what she wanted.

A few weeks before it had all got too much. Her receptionists job didn't pay a great deal, but Jim paid for everything when they went out and her parents gave her a free roof over her head and fed her. Since she spent little on clothes she'd banked almost all she'd earned. It amounted to a good few thousand dollars, so she'd started withdrawing it in cash a few hundred here, a few hundred there. It didn't take too long and she had the whole lot in cash in her holdall.

Then one night she went to bed, slept badly, got up early, tossed some underwear, a few tops, soap and a toothbrush on top of the cash, put on jeans, trainers and a sweater, grabbed an old baseball jacket and snuck out while everyone in the house was still asleep.

She'd briefly thought about leaving an explanatory note, an honest one, but although missing persons weren't missing persons until they'd been missing at least twenty four hours her pa and Jim's would have the local cops, at least, out looking for her immediately if she'd told them she'd run away. She thought, 'can grown ups run away anyway?'.

Whatever the legal position regarding runaways of her age if she said she'd left for good there would be pandemonium, and such was Jim senior's influence locally she felt quite sure that over twenty one or not, if discovered she'd be bundled into a squad car and returned to Phillips like a piece of lost property.

Not able to think of anything better she popped back in and scribbled 'things to do, see you later'. It might get her twenty four hours start anyway.

The first vehicle she'd seen was an old red Toyota, it had stopped and here she was.

When she'd laid awake at night imagining herself running away to San Francisco, it looked nice in magazines which is where most of her knowledge of the world came from, she'd taken it for granted she'd be picked up by a trucker and would have to be very careful, being frank with herself she'd been more than a bit fearful.

What she hadn't imagined was being whisked away by an English gentleman, feeling safe and having a laugh right from the get go, the door to the birdcage imprisoning her soul had simply swung open. Against everything she'd planned she told the whole story to Mike O'Brien, no detail omitted, no stone unturned, no personal thought denied. She felt strangely better for having done so too.

Mike tried to concentrate on the road but kept glancing at her and then having to force himself away from the holding power those luminous brown eyes exerted on his. Tanya's beautiful, soft, feminine eyes which had, for the first time in years lost all of their sadness, if not their soul, now sparkled with life. Mike imagined it was impossible to fall in love within a couple of hours, let alone first sight. Still grieving for Sarah and carrying guilt in his heart over both her and even Rachel, he could not conceive that he'd fallen in love, so quickly. Ridiculous. And yet, and yet, and yet, those eyes kept drawing him in.

When Tanya had poured out her heart to Mike, he realised that whether it was love, or something less, his emotions made him want to protect her, sweep her off her feet and make everything alright for her. He'd never been a rescuer and he didn't want to admit it was love, because it was too sudden, he didn't want to admit it was something less because that was to debase the feelings welling up inside him.

It was in fact love. That unaccountable life making, or life wrecking invisible force of nature. Sexually experienced, even skilful, largely thanks to Rachel, but never having experienced love before, real love, Mike was confused, abashed, uncertain, but he couldn't help admitting, wrong as it was, a feeling of joy that welled up inside him, like nothing he'd ever felt before, because he hadn't felt it before. He'd felt elements of it, protectiveness, caring, respect, but never the complete, uncontrollable rush of pure love. He wanted to grab a hold of it, but how do you hold on to the water leaping up from a fountain, you can't, but you can protect the fountain.

She'd been honest, maybe too honest, how many girls were virgins at twenty two? How many goddesses were virgins at twenty two? How many virgin goddesses wanted a gentle experienced man to lead them to intimate knowledge and intimate love?

Tanya wasn't entirely sure what she was feeling either. She'd felt vulnerable from the moment she'd raised her thumb. The idea of losing her virginity to someone who knew what to do turned her on, but could she really sleep with the first man she met? The 'I want to be wild and free' side of her mind screamed yes, the conservative side said wait 'he'll respect you more' and it also cast doubts about whether she should wait for the man she would love and marry and all the things she'd turned over in her mind a thousand times before.

'He's so nice though.'

She asked him what he was running away from.

"I thought that was coming."

"Fair's fair."

"Alright I won't lie to you, but if I tell you everything in detail it might sound a bit far fetched and what's more you don't want to get caught up in my problems, but I'll tell you the bones and then we can maybe decide if we can help each other.

"I drove a taxi in London for a living, I had an easy life, nice fun loving girlfriend, did a bit of cycling, swimming, dancing, life was undemanding but fun. One night some idiot left something, let's say incriminating in the back of my cab. When I got home I picked it up from the back seat took it indoors and read it. That information, which I wish I'd never seen made me a danger to some very powerful people and they've been after me ever since. An old friend, same age, similar looks loaned me his passport and his credit cards to get me started and I ran away to the USA.

"That's it in a nutshell, I found a place to stay in Lindsborg, managed to get some casual work and disappeared, or so I thought. I mean who goes to Lindsborg?"

"Funny you should have tried Phillips, no one goes in, no one goes out except maybe as far as Grand Island, and now me, I've gone out for good!"

Mike suddenly realised he'd been so taken up with the exchange of stories, she'd spoken much longer than him, that he was almost out of gas and suddenly swerved into the only gas station he'd seen for miles.

"Sorry, we're nearly out and I hadn't realised, getting stranded won't help either of us. You stay low, I'll fill up and pay and dash into the store for a few things and a bit of food, diners might not be a good idea for a while." 'Nor motels' he thought, but didn't say.

After filling up Mike disappeared inside the store for maybe five minutes, it seemed longer, Tanya worried, should she have trusted him? Was he even now on the phone? She thought about jumping out and hiding but just then he returned, one look into his eyes and her worries evaporated. Her instincts just said sound, he's a sound guy.

When he got back to the Landcruiser Mike handed a bag with sandwiches, chips (crisps to him), chocolate and bottled water to Tanya through the window and tossed a big bundle in the back.

"I don't do fizzy drinks but I can go back and get you something else if you like, sorry, I should have asked, all a bit rushed, mind's in a whirl, sorry."

"It's fine, you're fine, this is great, what's in the back?"

Mike pulled onto the highway.

"The guys after me must have a long reach. I left Lindsborg when people started asking questions about a missing English guy. I don't know how exactly, but I don't imagine it's a coincidence and I didn't want to find out so I high-tailed it out of there.

"From what you say it'll be twenty four hours at best before Jim Senior and your Dad have the highway patrol out, or whatever and five hours or so have gone already. So, both you and I want to keep a low profile, at least we can get out of state and no one knows whether you or I went north, south, east or west so we have some things going for us.

"Nonetheless the cops have resources, we don't, the odds aren't really in our favour, but the people looking for me probably aren't the same people who are looking for you, that probably helps, in addition anyone looking for me will know I'm alone, that might require explaining but trust me for the moment they'll believe I'm travelling alone. Anyone looking for you will be looking for a, sorry but it's true in a sense, lost girl alone in the world. As a happy looking couple we're already helping one another. Even if we look more like father and daughter!

"Motels and diners are a non starter though so in the back is a tent, sleeping bags, camping cooker, knife and a few utensils, fire lighter, that sort of thing and supplies, nothing fancy, the sort of stuff walkers carry. I'm not saying do as I say, but I'm kinda suggesting do as I do and we might, just might, disappear under the radar, what do you think?"

CHAPTER TWELVE – STURGIS

It hadn't taken them long, even travelling slowly, to reach Niobrara where the 14 became the 37 and a long low bridge crossed the mighty Missouri River, the boundary between Nebraska and South Dakota. Tanya was out of state, a momentous thing in itself, for her. With no particular place to go they settled into a comfortable silence.

Suddenly Tanya laughed out loud.

"We're in about as much trouble as two human beings can possibly get themselves into, pray tell, what's so funny?"

"Jim Junior, they'll blame him. Not just my parents, his parents will blame him too and when they grill him they'll find out just how well he doesn't know me. I know we have problems, but I wouldn't want to be in his shoes!"

Mike could see the funny side of that. They'd passed a camping and RV place shortly after the bridge, but it was too soon to stop. Suddenly the 37 made a ninety degree right turn. Did they want to go east? Mike pulled over, "we need a plan" he said, "first off are we a team?"

"Are The Braves a team?"

"I dunno, are they? I hope that's a bit like is The Pope Catholic? Yes, no?"

"We're a team sugar."

Tanya didn't know where that had come from, she'd never spoken to any man like that before, 'maybe, just maybe' she thought she was finding, no, expressing her true self, someone who'd been internalised and bottled up since adolescence.

"I studied maps of the USA a lot before I came here and I think if we go west more or less maybe north west, keeping north of the river anyway, we can get to Sturgis which is still out of state for you and might offer us a place to disappear"

"Explain."

"Well this Toyota has outlived its usefulness, if not now then pretty soon, the people trying to silence me will know what I'm driving. Sturgis may seem too close for comfort but on the open road in this we will be picked up, it's just a question of when.

"Pretty soon Sturgis will be hosting the Black Hills Motorcycle Rally, maybe it's even started, mostly Harleys but other American motorcycles too. Half a million bikers, maybe more, a six hundred acre campsite, bands like, I dunno Cher, through Steppenwolf, REO Speedwagon, that sort of thing, parties, revellers, if you can't find somewhere quiet to hide, get lost in the biggest crowd you can, I say.

"A lot of people people use a pick up like this to take their bikes to Sturgis, either on the back or on a trailer, don't want them getting dirty, it's all about show for some of them, this old thing has a tow hitch, I bet we could sell it then buy a bike. We'd disappear like tears on a rainy day, and we'd have transport to move on afterwards, just one of thousands of bikes heading out in different directions and they won't be looking for a couple of bikers, not my pursuers I shouldn't think, your folks see you as a biker chick?"

"No, doormat perhaps, obedient, pliable little angel maybe, but certainly not biker gal."

"Welcome to a whole new you then."

"The pickup won't get us enough for a bike but I have money, a ton of money actually."

"How much, five gees."

"Won't buy a Harley, I've got about thirty."

"Thirty dollars?"

"Thirty big ones as we say in the UK, that's another thirty gees to you."

"We're rich then!"

"No we're not rich, we both need a new wardrobe and helmets to go with the bike and when we find a place, we'll need to pay for camping, gas, food, we could blow the lot on a stand out bike, but we don't want to stand out, keep it to under ten thou I think, then we have twenty five to support ourselves and travel while we figure out our next move, and I think we deserve to live a little, who knows what tomorrow may bring."

"Isn't that a song?"

"Before your time sweet pea, but don't stop thinking about tomorrow."

"Now you're just playing games"

"Yes. Sturgis"

"Yes please driver."

Mike laughed, swung the old pickup around, headed west. They looked at each other and smiled, she reached out a hand, rested it on his thigh, left it there.

They could easily make Sturgis that day, but in order to avoid Interstate 90 they went a long way around and came at the town on the 34. A little way outside of town however they came across a broken down Harley and a guy on his knees, either praying or trying to fix it.

Mike pulled over. Something he wouldn't have happily done on the Interstate.

"What are you doing" whispered Tanya.

"We can't avoid people, especially the people we're hoping to mix with, problems are opportunities."

Mike jumped out "can we help you?"

"Just died, plenty of fuel, nothing visible that I can see."

"May I"

"Sure, if you know what you're doing."

"Enough to not make things worse."

Mike played with the S&S carb and the fuel lines. "Nice carb, well she's getting fuel." He pulled off a spark plug lead, got a plug spanner?"

"No sorry."

"Turn her over. I don't think you're getting a spark. Pretty certain it's coil or ignition failure, can't do anything without checking which and getting the parts. If we can get a deck plank, or ramp and some muscle I can drive you and the bike into town, they have a dealership. What do you think, fancy asking at that farm, see if they have something we can use and some helpers to get her up on the back, some straps'd be useful too."

"I'm happy to go ask if you're happy to wait."

"Sure thing"

Mike jumped back in the truck. "What's happening."

"Can't fix it at the roadside, he's going over to the farm to see if he can get help to get it up back."

"I thought we didn't want to be remembered."

"We don't but we can't ditch the truck and buy a bike without talking to people, lesser of two evils. That's an 88 Heritage Softail, it's twelve years old, broken down, but nothing much wrong with it. It's got a huge tank so great range, comfortable too, it's got bags and a luggage rack for our camping stuff, it's nice enough; we'd fit in here with a bike like that, but it's not special enough to stand out and it's gonna be in our price range."

"But it's not for sale is it?"

"Who knows what the guy is thinking, we're gonna need some help, so giving help..."

In the mirror Mike saw a small army approaching with what he knew back home as scaffold boards. He jumped out.

Five minutes later they were on their way, three up front and a Softail out back.

"What's your name? Forgot to ask."

"Billy"

"Funny"

Mike pulled out the pink slip and handed it to Billy. " You a Billy too then?"

"No but he was."

"Was?"

"Just haven't got around to making the change and now we want to sell it anyway don't we Carol?"

Tanya did a double take then mumbled "yes, we want a bike for Sturgis".

She looked strangely at Mike 'Blame Neil Sedaka' he thought but couldn't say anything.

"Actually I want to sell mine."

"Just because a coil failed or something like that?"

"Well you can tell I'm no mechanic, she's twelve years old now, I guess things are going to start to go wrong. The S&S is the only mod, my dealer did that. I fancy a custom bike American Iron Horse, Jesse James, West Coast Choppers..."

"What about a Bourget?"

"Yeah great man."

"You know those bikes look amazing, but, you got a long ride home?"

"Yeah Texas, but you gotta suffer for art they say."

"No you don't, what say we make you an offer for the Softail and include the truck, then you can drive your new toy home safe and immaculate, put a tarp over it. You'll still be able to walk when you get home too. I see they left you a couple of deck planks."

"I paid for those, but money's not the issue, oil business is doing okay."

"So, how much for the Heritage?"

"Ten gees."

"Eight gees and the truck."

"Trucks worth two hundred, not two gees."

"Think of the convenience, we drive straight to Sturgis Harley, you drive off to wherever you're staying with the truck, we're left with your non running bike, dependent on the dealer for the parts, you're off shopping for your dream bike at the shows right away before anyone else snaps up the best of them. Can't see Bourget or the like wanting part exchange either. Not so far from home.

"Not sure it's worth ten anyway, nine maybe, first year of production, not rare and you did say money was no issue..."

Tanya gave him a pleading look that would boil an iceberg.

How could he resist.

"There's something else you can do for me Billy" Tanya said, now it was Mike's turn to do a double take.

"My Dad's a cop and he's not happy about me running off with Vincent". 'Blame Don McLean' she thought.

"Too much of an age gap." Mike controlled his mirth, but barely.

"So if anyone asks, you bought it from a single dude, not a couple, paid cash, don't remember much about him, but definitely not English, pleeese."

It was too late to fix the bike that night, their first night under canvas, their first night sleeping together, not that they did much sleeping, nor anything else, talking took up most of the night.

"Where did Vincent come from?"

"Don McLean."

"Smart move on your part though let's hope we don't bump into Billy again, nice enough guy, but that bit is done now. The bike turns over, no bad sounds or signs, oil is clean, they're pretty solid you know and judging by the mileage this is the longest journey he's done. Bargain."

"So where did Carol come from?"

"Neil Sedaka, we gonna stick with those names for now?"

"Just for this location maybe, yes why not, new names new personas, just for Sturgis".

"Tomorrow we get the bike running, we can buy helmets at the dealership, then ride into Main Street and buy you some sexy biker girl outfits, wild one!"

Separate sleeping bags, but they stripped down to their underwear without embarrassment and Tanya went to sleep with her head on Mike's chest. 'This could get to be a habit for first nights' he thought. He looked at her until he couldn't keep his eyes open any longer. 'Thank goodness for sheer exhaustion' he thought as he drifted off.

Although the Black Hills Motorcycle Rally started in 1938 with just nine bikes the year 2000 would be the official 60th anniversary due to the war years and suchlike. Six hundred thousand people would turn up to party. Fortuitously Mike and Tanya had arrived on the Wednesday before the two week extravaganza got going and although they were far from from being the only early birds, it did mean they got a pitch for the tent without much trouble, despite not booking in advance. Small tent anyhow, and now there was no truck to take up space either.

Mike was also able to borrow a multi meter and some tools, buy a new ignition coil and just like that they were mobile, on just the two wheels this time. Sturgis was a bit of a blur for both of them, parties, drinking, singing, concerts, shopping for everything from bikinis to T shirts, lacy underwear the like of which Tanya had never worn before to chaps, boots, gloves and leather jackets.

Mike was careful to never ride with any level of alcohol in his bloodstream whatsoever, life was complicated enough without injuries, nor did he have a licence or insurance, a fact he was only too aware of, care was the order of the day, great care, for both their sakes. The concerts, parties and the atmosphere were incredible and fears about being found evaporated for two whole glorious weeks, lost in the crowds and looking just like everyone else, apart from tattoos maybe.

On the second night they zipped their sleeping bags together into one big one and slept completely naked. With their hands they gently explored each others' bodies, Tanya experiencing sensations and feelings entirely new and completely outside her experience for all that she'd experimented a little, alone at home, in her single bed.

On the third night they made love, which Mike realised was also a new experience for him too. He'd had his teenage fumblings, he'd had exciting, wild sexual experiences with Rachel, he'd cared deeply for Sarah, but he'd never been moved the way he was now.

It wasn't just because Tanya was a virgin, or that he relished giving her new experiences, though he did, it wasn't just that she was the most beautiful girl, blossoming into the most beautiful woman he'd ever seen, though she was, it wasn't just that he wanted to protect and cherish her, though he did, it was all of those things and more, it was the trick nature plays on most mortals once in their life at least, something the cynical call chemistry, but which is in fact more of a slow motion explosion shattering all the certainties of before.

At the end of two virtually carefree, wild weeks of fun, ride outs and concerts, and even meeting real people, some of whom might prove useful one day, it was time to discuss a plan of action. Mike had already got a small notebook where he'd made a list of names of people they had met and all the information he could glean about them. Tanya wondered what he was doing it for and eventually her curiosity got the better of her.

"In normal circumstances it would have been easier to exchange names, phone numbers or email addresses, but we can't do that, so if we ever need to turn to anyone we've met here for help, if we know their full name, where they live, who they work for, family details, that kind of thing we might be able to track them down again."

"OK I get that, but who here can help us and when they find out we're not who we said we were why would they want to help us?"

"Well, the world is made up of all kinds of people and shared experiences can build a bond, as can shared passions and shared concerns. The American Motorcycle Community you might call it is very diverse. New top of the range Harleys don't come cheap, custom bikes like the ones our friend Billy was looking for can run to six figures, especially if they're bespoke with the best of everything.

"So here we have everything from biker gangs with somewhat shady, probably criminal contacts and leanings through to professional doctors, lawyers, political activists, engineers and artisans who can make things, millionaire businessmen; actually with half a million people or more pretty much all life is here.

"I've been as helpful and as sociable as it's safe to be and there are a few people here who I'm sure would sympathise with us if they knew the truth. No point giving anything away now, but the time may come when I, anyway, have to roll the dice and you will want to be yourself again, your real identity, IRS, drivers licence the lot, marriage licence, who knows."

"If you can't marry then I won't be!"

"That's lovely to hear and I love you too, I hope we can make a life, but we have more problems to overcome than just about any other couple. I'm effectively a fugitive, remember.

"Anyway we need to sit down and make a new plan Sam."

"Sam?"

"Hop on the bus Gus, Paul Simon, but it's about leaving your lover so totally inappropriate, sorry, but we do need to make a plan."

"Back to songs for names then, maybe I will be Samantha for the next bit and you can be Gus, so there!"

"I think I'm fine with Gus and you're bewitching, but a plan, people are drifting away, only the diehards left now, we were lost in a crowd ,now, soon anyway, no crowd any more, so it's where to and why?

"What were your ideas when you left home?"

"My dreams were all about San Francisco and University. I did well at school and I can access my certificates and grades. Of course I've been in work, not straight out of school, but maybe I could get in."

"One place is as good as another for me, I had to leave Lindsborg which appeared to be small, anonymous, the last place anyone would look and that didn't work, being lost amongst hundreds of thousands seemed to work so why not three million?"

"You know a lot of stuff for a taxi driver don't you!"

"Never underestimate a London cabby, cab drivers have won Mastermind."

"What's that?"

"UK television quiz show, we meet so many people, we get to learn loads about peoples' way of life, their interests, hobbies, places they've been, want to go to, we're just soaking up information all the time, well, the talkative ones like me are anyway. It teaches you to be able to communicate with every type of person too, which is why I rubbed along OK with the Hells Angels and Outlaws to the doctors, lawyers, oilmen, millionaires and CEOs.

"Of course finding out too much got me into this predicament, I won't say mess because it brought me to you, but this predicament in the first place. Generally speaking though, knowledge is power, remember that if we're ever forced to separate.

"So, San Francisco it is, not keen to use the Interstate, time we bought a map and planned more carefully."

CHAPTER THIRTEEN – BACK ON THE ROAD AGAIN

It would be possible to reach San Francisco, using Interstate 80, even cruising at laid back comfortable speeds, in under thirty hours of riding. As comfortable as the Softail might be for a motorcycle, seven hours in the saddle, say three in the morning and four in the afternoon would be plenty. On reflection Mike thought, best reverse that, or even start early and do five hours in the morning as he thought they'd be going through Nevada into California later where it gets pretty hot.

First Wyoming and Utah, great scenery. Theoretically four and a half to five days would be comfortable, but by avoiding the Interstate they'd better allow a couple of weeks. Anyway, the open road, a tent, a beautiful girl, well, woman now, coming into her own; let's have the best of times whilst we can, because the worst of times could return at any time.

In broad brushstrokes the plan involved getting on their old friend the 14 a little way west of Sturgis to the Yellowstone National Park, lots of tourists at this time of year, now the second half of August. Then take the 20 down to Idaho Falls and the 20 and 26 to The Craters Of The Moon National Monument. Then the 20 again, and very briefly Interstate 84 to Boise, unless they could find some very small back roads.

The map was at a scale that didn't show every last detail. Anyway, they'd venture into Oregon before taking the 20 to a tiny unincorporated community called Riley, the 395 south to Lake Abert and Goose Lake. Below Goose Lake they'd take the 299 to Canby, now in California at least. From there the 139 and 39 to Klanarth Falls, the 66 to Cascade-Siskiyon National Monument, the 96 to the six Rivers National Forest and the 299 to the west coast.

It was not the obvious route from Sturgis to San Francisco, lots of going north and south. However, it would be cooler than heading straight across Nevada and their final destination would not be obvious to anyone who saw and remembered them. Once at the coast they'd largely follow it south on the 101 and 1 into San Francisco, thus fulfilling the first of Tanya's dreams.

Mike tore a page from his notebook, made notes of road numbers, and directions, towns that were large enough to feature on signposts that were in the right way, even if they weren't visiting them.

He scotch taped the information to the tank in front of him for easy reference, but kept the roll of tape. The route would have to be removed from the bike anytime they left it unattended.

Other aspects of the plan were still somewhat hazy. Mike assumed that since term often started at the beginning of October in many British Universities that Tanya might be able to start at University, Berkeley or Stamford. He wasn't aware that term had just started, nor did he understand the admissions process, nor the costs. These things being somewhat down the road a bit he'd taken them granted.

On day one they rode to a place called the Lazy R Campground and Cabins in Ranchester on the 14 in Wyoming. By car taking the most direct route they'd have done it in three hours but taking the slow road, stopping when they felt like it, needed a rest or food, or just wanted to enjoy places they passed through they took a lazy seven hours.

When planning the ride Mike had fantasised about camping at the side of the road, away from everyone and everything, under the stars. It was a romantic notion and maybe if they were out in the Nevada desert somewhere he could have pulled it off. He soon realised that camping by the road was a non starter. Every bit of land is owned by someone, alone they'd be vulnerable to crime and he felt the need to protect Tanya, he also wanted her to have proper facilities, even though he'd bought a folding trenching tool and toilet tissue.

A tent by the side of the road might prompt an enquiry from a passing patrol car too, a tent on a campground, no problem. Throw in showers and shopping it was pretty much what might be called a no brainer even though he hated the term. That they managed to sneak a shower together in the ladies facilities assuaged any disappointment.

Both aching from longer hours in the saddle than they were used to, the hot water and the feel of their bodies entwined, soapy and scented brought them back to their happy place. The only problem with public showers and public camping with thin walls and thin fabric was that you really had to keep your voices down, both during intimacy and during any discussion that might involve being on the run from something.

They paid when they entered, explaining they'd be away early in the morning, asked where they were going they simply answered Yellowstone, it was logical enough and vague enough, asked where they'd come from they said Sturgis, which of course meant they could have been from anywhere. The receptionist could see they only had eyes for each other so she forgave the unreadable scrawl in the book and sent them to their pitch. It was a routine Samantha and Gus would hone to perfection as campsites came and went.

Day two saw them at Moose Creek Flat, Montana, a little shy of their day's target destination of Big Sky. The National Forest, the mountains and the river were beautiful, there were still many wild flowers in bloom. They'd have been tempted to try the white water rafting on the river, but, with the need for a low profile, meetings with as few people as possible and to be as forgettable as possible. It wasn't easy.

Tanya would do most of the talking so that Mike's accent wouldn't be a cause for comment. People were always polite to her you don't ask personal questions of a beautiful young woman with her boyfriend standing there. 'Too old, the lucky Bastard' some thought, Mike was oblivious. They had their responses down to a fine art in just two days, the only thing they couldn't get around was that Tanya was far from being forgettable, their hope lay in the fake name and the fact that as far as Mike knew anyone looking for him did not know that he was now half of a most memorable, stand out couple.

The sexy outfits that were de rigueur at Sturgis weren't such a bonus now. Again they hit the road early. Enjoying the scenery, stopping often, day three took them only as far as Idaho falls. Four hours in the saddle although they could have gone faster, but an eight hour day enjoying stops, scenery and kisses. Nonetheless it was early afternoon when they checked into the Snake River RV Park. Luckily Gus and Samantha had left reception when they bumped into a couple from Sturgis who knew them as Carol and Vincent.

Good to have some company though, the four agreed to have dinner together, anonymity not being a possibility and anyway William and Charlotte were already prominent in Mike's notebook. William was a practising Human Rights Lawyer with contacts in Amnesty and other organisations, Charlotte was a freelance journalist, but she'd been published in the Washington Post, New York Times and was a regular columnist for the LA Times. They lived in Santa Monica.

At first the conversation was about where the two couples were going, not a subject Carol and Vincent wanted to pursue, so they were as vague as possible, but managed to get the conversation around, first to Charlotte's career and then William's. Like Carol and Vincent, William and Charlotte were soulmates who'd met when Charlotte was working on an article about abuses by the church in Central America and other strongly Catholic places such as Ireland, and William was representing some of the victims. They soon found they shared a passion for each other as well as a passion for justice and helping others.

Despite their high flying educational and career successes, William and Charlotte were not at all pretentious. Tanya relaxed and let slip some of her story and some of her hopes regarding a university education. Already politics, human rights and journalism had all started to interest her. Maybe even law. She revealed that her parents had held her back, even that her family had tried to engineer a marriage she didn't want, then as suddenly as she'd started she clammed up. Nonetheless William and Charlotte enquired gently about her high school grades and proffered business cards without asking for any details in return, saying they'd be happy to help in any way. Nice folks, as Americans say.

Back at the tent Mike made copious notes and copied down the details from the business cards which he left with Tanya before lying back and inviting her to lay her head on his chest again. She started to apologise for letting her mouth run away with her.

"No stop, you were brilliant, we had to say something about ourselves in that situation, it would have looked odd otherwise. They're not the sort of people to call your parents, they're all about rights and you're a grown woman, whatever your parents think.

Not only that, it at least partly explains you being with an older man and in the end it was too late in the evening to start a new story about my life before it all wound up. So I was kept out of it, with no need to lie to them. I'd thought that they might be handy contacts to have when we met them at Sturgis, but there was no opportunity for such an intimate conversation there. No, tonight was just possibly a stroke of good fortune and even if not, no harm done I think."

Mike had hoped to make the Craters of The Moon National Monument the day before but 'plans exist to be changed' he thought, so now, having stopped not far short it was only a couple of hours or so ride away, but they could explore the extinct volcanic landscape and have some, another ghastly expression, quality time together. They hadn't spent precious resources on helmet intercoms so time in the saddle was uncommunicative although they'd agreed Tanya would tap Mike on his right shoulder if she wanted or needed to stop.

Mike wanted to savour every moment with Tanya that he could get. As well as things had been going he wasn't confident that they wouldn't become separated of necessity at some point. Not realising it was already too late for her to get into Berkeley or Stanford this year he wanted to get to San Francisco reasonably quickly, yet the uncertainty of what would happen when they got there meant that in his heart he wished this journey would never end.

Even taking detours, making stops to admire the scenery and to kiss and cuddle as if both of them were new young lovers and then cruising slowly they still arrived at Lava Flow Campsite mid morning and to their delight were able to pitch tent well away from anyone else.

They passed the day making love, talking, making love again, taking a walk, making love and eventually eating. For all the passion they still managed to discuss things of consequence. Mike asked Tanya about her preferred university, what course she wanted to do and said he'd get her there in time, which elicited some amusement from Tanya who had researched further education long ago.

"Finally something you don't know anything about!" She teased.

"There's no way I can get into university this year. Term has already started."

"No!"

"Yes, then there's the application process, acceptance, FEES, which I couldn't afford even if you gave me the rest of your money, which you're going to need.

"I'm going to have to get a job and that means no more off grid, as you call it, for me. I may be able to get some sort of classes to improve my chances of acceptance next year, and I'm going to have to save. I need to get a message to Mom, she'll be frantic, I need to let her know I'm alive and well and that I'm pursuing the life I want. It would help if I can get her onside. Tell her if she wants to see me in future then they all have to give up on controlling who I marry, where I work, whether I choose an education and they've got to leave me in peace and not chase after me.

"The right letter will have Mom see sense and she'll get her way with the others in the end, with the exception of me she always has, in fact she controlled me too for the longest time but finally she met her match in her daughter I think, it just took a while. So if Mom commands they don't look for me, they don't look for me. All the same we need to get the letter posted by someone else as far as possible from any place we've been, Whether that's, Seattle, DC, New York, Dallas, no matter. That way if your people, seems strange calling them that, but if your people find out you've been travelling with me they'll start looking in completely the wrong area."

"You really are starting to think like a fugitive too aren't you, but you're right and I was feeling guilty about your folks, just didn't want to express it and risk upsetting you."

That evening Tanya took some paper from Dave's notebook and over a couple of very thoughtful hours put it all down for her mom. She didn't hold back on the detail, the fact that she would not be controlled and that her life was her life. Tough love would be the only way, any hint of weakness and the family would seek to find her and persuade her to do what they thought was sensible.

She made clear that as much as she loved them, if they wanted a relationship in the future they would respect her wishes now, no negotiation they'd had their way all her life and she was one hundred percent resolved. Let go now and all is not lost, come after me you'll regret it is what it really said although not in exactly those words. Her mom would see it was best to cut their losses. It would do.

The letter was carefully put away in a zip up pocket until they could find an envelope and find someone to mail it from a far off place.

Boise, the capitol of Idaho looked like a really nice place to stop next, but it really was too few miles. The city of Burns didn't appeal, if they were going to stop in a city it ought to be Boise. There were two small unincorporated communities, one Juntura, Spanish for junction and on the junction of two rivers looked possible, but Mike thought they could get as far as a place called Riley. It was also an unincorporated tiny community, they'd be noticed, but not so many people there to notice them, 'everything is a compromise' Mike thought.

At the lazy pace they travelled it might take eight hours or more, but it was mostly westward and about time they made some distance, Riley became the next target destination. The place was basically a Post Office they couldn't use to send Tanya's letter, and a General Store. On the other hand they could buy provisions and probably risk one night camping by the road a little way out of town, if you could call two buildings a town. Mike's fantasy might be realised for one night anyway, camping under the stars, just the two of them, no camp ground just this once.

They'd be about two thirds of the way to the west coast, but well north of San Francisco, maybe they'd risk the grandeur and beauty of the coastal route south later. The feeling of being pursued was beginning to seem unreal, but Mike knew that in his case at least he was unlikely to be forgotten, by whoever didn't want him running around with the knowledge he had in his head.

The scenery was less beautiful now, but the time spent together was precious, both relished every moment. They camped roadside in the middle of nowhere effectively, having bought supplies at the store, where a bored shopkeeper had wanted to chat. They explained they had come from Sturgis and were on their way back to California. Back to California made sense and was of course a red herring, coming from Sturgis on a Harley, that made sense, they were as friendly and talkative as they were able to be and unbeknownst to them it saved their bacon.

A local cop who would normally have questioned a couple of bikers camping by the road heard at the store that they were a nice couple, Samantha and Gus, professionals probably, on their way home from Sturgis. 'That's ok then, no need to disturb them' he thought. They'll be gone on their way in the morning anyhow, which they were. Their lovemaking was becoming more passionate and more varied as Tanya wanted to learn and to give as well as to receive. Despite the small tent, both felt completely satisfied, at peace and happy, more a sense of deep down joy that expunged all worry, for now.

Mike thought about stopping at the City of Sisters, so called, although with a population of around two thousand it was a very small city, he thought they really should go further though; as wonderful as the journey was they were far enough into it now to start thinking earnestly about an end game, finding a place they could stay longer term so that Tanya could get her job and eventually start her studies.

As for himself, Mike wasn't sure what he would do, he felt so strongly about spending the rest of his life with Tanya that he started to wonder how he could make this all go away.
Should he go public, in that way there'd be no point in trying to silence him, would there, maybe? Would any media outlet take him seriously? Should he give himself up and trust the authorities to do the right thing, it might involve prison time though and prison time when national security was involved, well, that might be a very long time indeed, especially in the USA.

In the end they rode to the equally attractive sounding City of Sweet Home, Oregon, with it's attractive lakes and mountains where they opted for a motel, for a change, and where, having showered together, made love and showered again they decided to treat themselves to a proper meal out.

They went back the way they'd come, to The Point Restaurant on Foster Lake which they'd passed earlier. It looked nice and it was, so was the location, Mike had a steak with all the trimmings, too much for an Englishman really, he still hadn't become accustomed to American portion sizes even after all this time, largely as a result of eating out very, very infrequently. Tanya had seafood and they shared a home made raisin sour cream pie for dessert. It was certainly the best meal they'd had since meeting and it came with a bonus.

Their server was not just professionally friendly but, genuinely friendly. It came out in conversation that her husband was a trucker who'd be taking a load to Austin, Texas, leaving the following morning. Tanya explained that she'd left home and that she was old enough to make her own decisions, whatever her dad thought, but she wanted her mom to know she was ok. She said she'd written a letter, but didn't want to mail it herself in case her dad came looking for her, "do you think your husband would mail it for me in Austin?"

"Sure honey he's tough looking on the outside, buttercream on the inside, I tell him this has to be mailed in Austin, it gets mailed in Austin. Reliable as that Harley of yours."

No one mentioned they'd bought it as a non runner.

"I've got the letter in my pocket, but no envelope yet."

"Hang fire I'll get one from the office you can seal it and address it, I promise it will be mailed."

"Your tip is gonna include the mailing and a big, bonus."

"Really, it's a pleasure, don't often get to talk to such a nice couple, English gents are rare round here too" she said flashing her broadest smile at Mike who told her she was a sweetheart.

Tanya visibly relaxed, that letter had been weighing on her mind more than she knew.

They thought about staying on the same route to Newport on the coast but decided Florence would be just as easy about six to eight hours depending on speed and stops. From Florence they could do Klamath in a day, travelling down the coast and Klamath was across the state line into California. The home of Tanya's dreams and a lot of other young people's dreams too.

So it was that on day seven they rode to Florence and on day eight celebrated their arrival in California. Day nine would take them to Santa Rosa. From Klamath to Santa Rosa on the inland 101 was possible in about five, five and a half hours at their customary, leisurely pace but they took the 1 down the coast and made a full day of it. The coast road was stunning and both, quietly, unable to converse whilst riding, reflected to themselves that this amazing adventure was coming to an end with who knows what to follow.

At Santa Rosa they found a KOA camp ground between Santa Rosa and San Francisco, San Francisco North really where they could access local newspapers and magazines and make a list of accommodation to rent. On the morrow they would shower early, put on their most respectable clothes and ride into town to try and find a place to rent with no references and no ID!

CHAPTER FOURTEEN – SAN FRANCISCO

Before setting off for San Francisco that morning Mike and Tanya took stock of their finances and prioritised the accommodation ads by cheapest first.

They had divided the cash between them, partly so it wouldn't all be in one bag, or one place; in the event of a robbery they might not lose it all. Time to take stock.

"Let's check how much we have left. We had about twenty seven thousand after buying the bike, that must be about four weeks ago. You count up what you've got in your bag and I'll do the same."

"Twelve thousand and fifty."

"Crikey, that was quick!"

"A lot of people still trust cash where I come from, even to buy cars, I got used to checking the cash and counting out large amounts."

"OK just a sec. Seven thou. four hundred and change. That's nearly nineteen and a half left from the roughly thirty five we started with. You're not a cheap date you know that!"

"Huh, worth every cent."

"You are actually and more, I reckon we spent around two and a half at Sturgis on clothes, helmets, fuel, food, concerts, then we probably spent about five hundred a day on average for ten days travelling, camping grounds, fuel food, treats.

"However the bike is an asset we won't need for long if we play our cards right, and there's always the risk of getting pulled over with no ID, no insurance and no licence; it's a liability really and public transportation in and around San Francisco is good, those wonderful old trams. We'll use the bike whilst we hunt down a place to stay then take it to the main dealership, hopefully they'll give us a fair price, but they'll expect a healthy profit. Still we've got the pink, we lose a liability and get something back at least."

After an optimistic start the day turned into something of a disappointment that went from bad to worse. No one seemed to want to rent a place, or even a room to a couple of bikers with no ID, no references and no bank account. By four pm Mike suggested they take another approach. Let's see what we can get for the bike, we may have to use cheap hotels until we can get your ID and get you a job.

"I'm an idiot, I emptied my bank account, didn't think I'd want the check book and card, I've got a drivers licence at home too."

"By now your mom will have the letter and will think you're in Texas."

"I'll have to call her, if I do it at the right time of day no one else will pick up. I'll promise to give her regular calls and news, but only if she keeps her mouth shut, she can mail my stuff. I know it's a risk, but honestly she'll quite like a bit of a girly, mom daughter conspiracy and she'll know if she breaks trust she'll risk losing contact completely."

"I think you're right. As far as we know, no one knows the guy you're travelling with is me, so to speak, wanted fugitive of good character with no previous! One of us needs to be on the grid, it's hard to get anything done otherwise. You have your dreams and ambitions to consider too.

"OK, we have a plan, let's take the bike to the shop and see what we can get for it, before the day gets any older."

The first part of that plan went badly too. The manager was suspicious that they didn't have ID, but they did have the slip, the bike could be registered, they didn't seem like the kind of people that would have stolen it. Even so, he offered a paltry four thou., half what they'd paid for a non runner, and said that he'd have to clear it with the boss who wasn't in today, so they'd have to come back tomorrow and the final nail, "bring your bank details."

Actually Tanya could remember her bank details by heart, but if the money was paid in there she couldn't access it until she got her stuff from her mom ,who she hadn't even called yet and the name on her bank account didn't match the name she'd given. Oh what tangled webs we weave.

It seemed hopeless, no place to stay and they couldn't even sell the bike, at which moment.

"Vince, Carol, what ya doin' dudes?"

Mike and Tanya turned as one.

"Whoa! Monkey! Hey man, just selling our ride."

Monkey was short for monkey wrench, his real name forgotten by everyone except himself, his mother, his sister and a couple of close friends and his bank manager. Monkey was a Hells Angel member who fixed bikes, could fix anything, any resemblance to a monkey was coincidental despite the long hair, beard and black chest hair that sprung up from his t shirt.

"Why?"

"Green-backs; homeless, job less, what else! What you doing here?"

"Parts, I use after-market a lot but some people want original, occasionally original is better, not always though, but some folks just want that. I'm in here once or twice a week. These shysters know me. What they offer you?"

"Four!"

"Oh man, even I'd give you five."

"Listen, you got time to have a beer with us."

"Sure, I'll just pick up my gear, it's already ordered and boxed, help me get it to the truck and you can follow me to the clubhouse."

Mike and Tanya had met Monkey at Sturgis, the kind of Hells Angel who risked getting the Angels a good name! At the clubhouse there were a few other faces they recognised who acknowledged them but the three friends sat in a corner with a growing collection of empty bottles in front of them on the table and talked.

Maybe the drinking loosened tongues, maybe Mike felt confiding in someone he liked, and who maybe wasn't always what most people would see as the right side of the line regarding the law himself, was the only way forward in this current predicament. He was operating outside the law himself, even if Tanya wasn't.

By the end of the evening Monkey knew almost as much about Mike as Tanya did, he didn't care why someone was after Mike, he liked the guy, OK he was an illegal, but hell the Brits we're alright, he'd been over to the Bulldog, Mike wasn't HA but he could be considered almost a bro. Mike and Tanya added five thou to the war chest, lost the Harley and found themselves a home, well a room into the bargain. Luck restored. Monkey's sister had kicked her man out and even though he'd become more of a liability than a contributor, sub letting a room to a nice couple Monkey had vouched for would sure help with the bills.

Josey knew they were good for it too, Monkey had phoned and told her he'd bought their ride so they had five thou. That she knew of to see them through until they started earning. Given Mike and Tanya had no other options a deal was agreed on the phone, room unseen, house unseen. Five hundred dollars a month.

Mike had spoken to Josey direct on the phone after Monkey laid out the proposition, the cheapest room Mike and Tanya had looked at earlier was seven hundred dollars. "Are you sure?" he'd asked her.

"Sure, I wouldn't have advertised it, might have got any old weirdo coming round, this way I get someone safe, quick and five hundred cash every month tax free, good for you, good for me."

They'd verbally shaken then and there.

Mike and Tanya were amazed to find Josey living in a really nice house in an area known as Russian Hill, not far from Fisherman's Wharf to the north, Japantown to the south and the ferry building and Oakland Bay bridge to the east. Mike privately found it a highly amusing coincidence since he still at least half believed it was Russians who'd kidnapped him and were even now trying to find him again.

The tramway with overhead power lines and the cable cars as they're known which are pulled by cables in a slot in the road were all around, plus buses, there were also trendy bars and cafes; not cheap, they'd have to make sure they didn't let the lifestyle run away with them. The room was nice with an iron bedstead, Josey was putting fresh linen on the bed when Monkey dropped them off. She invited them in and went straight back to making their bed.

Josey was wearing a slightly the worse for wear strappy T shirt that hung off her as she leaned forwards and revealed a lot of side boob plus a tattoo that read 'Property of Mike'. Tanya saw Mike looking and dug him in his side with an elbow. Josey, bending over the bed, also noticed.

"Sorry, interesting tattoo."

"I was HA too, actually you never really leave, those kind of tats, pretty common in the club, some of the slutty girls just have 'Property Of HA' anyway Mike was actually the one before last, I guess I'll do something about it one day, unless I find a Mike I like!"

"This one's taken"

"Shame, aren't you the lucky girl!"

There was no malice or jealousy, they'd all rub along just fine. Mike's better luck had fully returned. Still, he wasn't sure he'd be able to get work, but they had enough in the kitty to last for many months at this price, Tanya could certainly get work, but he'd have to pull his weight too somehow, they didn't need to simply get by, they needed university fees, savings and a plan to somehow get Mike papers; residency, drivers licence, passport, an identity that would allow him to live. One thing at a time eh.

Tanya had to wait until the next morning to call her mom. She tilted the phone a little away from her ear having invited Mike to listen in.

"You're the one taking all the risks, you'd better listen, it might reassure you."

Josey had gone to work, she was in fact a qualified pharmacist, hence the nice home although as she'd said herself, it had been easier with two incomes until her last boyfriend, something in finance, got the coke habit.

"Mom."

"Tanya, what the..."

"Mom, just listen OK and don't interrupt till I finish or I'll hang up."

It was a long conversation and not without some tricky moments to navigate.

"Are you with someone?"

"No Mom I'm not with anyone"

"How did you get to San Francisco? Why did your letter come from Austin?"

"Greyhound and because I didn't want you to know where I was, actually I didn't want Dad or the Jims to know."

"You know Jim Junior is heartbroken don't you?"

"No, he isn't, his pride is hurt, that's all."

"Look Mom, I didn't have much of a plan when I left but I do now and I've grown up quickly the last month or so. So here's the deal, you work with me, you send me what I need. In return you get regular phone calls, you get to hear about what I'm doing, what job I get, when I start uni, what I'm studying, exam results, we get to be best friends again, but, you don't come here, you don't tell Dad or anyone else, that's anyone else, you don't say to Dad ooh I fancy a vacation in San Francisco, no games and we'll see how it goes. Any hint of trouble I will move on again and next time I won't contact you."

Tanya got her drivers licence, social security number, her high school diploma, her check book and bank card and a promise of help if she needed anything else. Tanya suggested that a reference on Jim senior's headed paper would be useful, but her mom would have to steal the paper and type the reference herself. Which shouldn't be too difficult Tanya assured her.

Her reference arrived several days after everything else and when Tanya checked her bank she found Sandra had paid in two thousand dollars. She had a little cry.

Not long after Tanya secured a job as a receptionist at the Marriott Marquis, there was a cable car about every eighteen minutes, but it was not much more than a mile on foot, she could keep in shape and save the fare.

Within days she was as popular at the hotel as she'd been at the Auto showroom. Within six months the conference manager would leave to have a baby, the management already having sufficient confidence in Tanya, who always helped out at conferences anyway, would put her in charge temporarily to see if she could handle it with a bit of help. When the Conference Manager eventually made the decision not to return but to be a full time mom Tanya would get the job permanently. With Sandra paying into her daughter's bank account surreptitiously whenever she could savings for university fees started to accumulate.

Mike meanwhile, after some discussion, got a cash in hand job spannering for Monkey. Mike already had some basic knowledge, enough to check that broken down Harley for fuel and a spark, he basically knew a bit about how things worked, but he learned a great deal extra from Monkey about electronics, valve clearances, gearboxes, wheel bearings and much more.

Monkey found Mike a quick learner and was soon able to leave the simpler jobs to him entirely. This meant he was able to take on double the work load, since many of the jobs that came in were relatively simple fixes, or service items, which Mike could do unaided, whilst Monkey got on with the more elaborate welding, fabricating and customising that brought in the really big bucks, but which previously kept getting interrupted by the small, bread and butter jobs from his established customers he couldn't afford to turn away.

With over nineteen thousand dollars cash plus another five from the Softail Mike and Tanya had started out with around twenty four thousand dollars, banking large amounts of cash might look strange, they'd already agreed to pay Josey in cash but even paying cash for absolutely everything else on top, given Mike was paid in cash and business was booming their cash reserves were increasing not decreasing and all of Tanya's wages which were paid into her bank were untouched, she worried that might look strange too, so she opened some savings accounts and moved money into those, which also accrued a bit of interest on top.

With, not infrequent, donations coming in from Sandra too it was beginning to look as if the goal of having a proper budget for university within well under a year might actually be achievable. Time to think about the application process.

CHAPTER FIFTEEN – MANHUNT

Whilst these fortuitous events had been taking place, other people were less happy, people including the President of the USA, the Prime Minister of Great Britain, the head of the CIA and the head of MI6. Their lackeys Kevin Donohue and Sean Hobbs, whose reputations as favourite sons in their respective spy rings were severely tarnished, with their bosses anyway, were also highly frustrated. Most people in those secretive organisations still had no idea what those two were working on and knew better than to ask.

Given that Donohue and Hobbs knew who they were looking for, knew broadly where he'd fled to, knew exactly what he looked like, knew the name on the passport he'd used, how on earth could they have failed to pick him up? It was September now, the guy had fled in January for chrissakes. More than eight months! Donohue was more convinced than ever that O'Brien was working for a foreign power.

Even Hobbs had a few doubts; he had painstakingly analysed O'Brien's entire life, parents, birth, education, work history, he'd looked at every holiday the man had ever taken, his friends, his girlfriends, his grandparents, aunts and uncles and the political affiliations, where known, of all these disparate people and had still found no evidence whatsoever of treachery.

If it was a cover, it was a damn good one, if Mike O'Brien had been a sleeper how the hell would he have been inserted, even his parents and grandparents were perfectly normal people. O'Brien himself had traced his own family tree back to the eighteen hundreds for the fun of it and kindly left his research at home to be scrutinised.

One grandfather had served with distinction in the Essex regiment in World War One, not an Irish regiment, the O'Briens had been in England for generations. The other grandfather had been a conscientious objector, but had nevertheless served in the Royal Army Medical Corps. Both grandfathers had served in World War Two as well, being in East London they'd been on the receiving end of Hitler's blitz, one had been a fire spotter, the other an air raid warden. O'Brien's father had served in the RAF, his mother had walked to school during the blitz, her parents declining to evacuate her and had gone to work for the Ministry Of Defence straight after school. Hardly enemies of the state any of them.

The one and only thing that stuck out as odd was how an ordinary London cabby could escape and evade for so long without training, it was the only thing that didn't add up and it was the only thing that mattered to Hobbs's partner Donohue, whose mind was made up.

A crisis meeting was held at The Agency headquarters at Langley with both Tenet and Dearlove in attendance and Blair and Clinton available by hotline. A plan was made which no one except Kevin Donohue, its instigator, was especially keen on, it involved a great deal of dishonesty and no small number of compromises. However, given no one had any better suggestions...

In a nutshell Mike O'Brien would be branded a serial killer in the USA and his photograph circulated in national media. A plan fraught with difficulty, potential future lawsuits and operational problems too. The media story would have to be very light on detail, because victims' names and the circumstances of the supposed murders would be too easy to check. In the UK where the alleged offences took place the story was the subject of an injunction on national security grounds, so it couldn't run in Great Britain, but that alone made an enormous stink of falsehood.

Nonetheless the story was published in the USA, Donohue anticipated an immediate arrest, the good people of America wouldn't harbour a serial killer, every cop in the country would have the picture, there were orders not to shoot, they wanted O'Brien alive for questioning, however, there was a worry that a trigger happy cop might disobey, after all a serial killer, if they look like they're trying to get away you just shoot the fuckers don't you. Hobbs wondered if some American Law Enforcement Officers signed up precisely for the thrill of shooting someone dead, but even he accepted it would probably be a very small minority. Still, Americans and their guns.

In Los Angeles journalist Charlotte Standing saw the release and immediately recognised Mike O'Brien as the person she knew as Vince. She also immediately recognised the incongruities, the lack of detail, she smelled a rat. She asked her colleagues what they knew, none of them knew anything. She took a photocopy to discuss with Bill, told no one she'd met the suspect, or that he was travelling under the name Vincent with a beautiful young woman named Carol.

"Bill, this is going to appear in tomorrow's papers."

"Let's see; my goodness, Charlotte, that's Vincent!"

"Looks like his real name is Mike O'Brien, I can't quite see him as a serial killer though can you?"

"No, but I guess they're very credible these people and there's that young girl to think of I'll call the cops, or have you done that?"

"No I haven't and I don't think you should. In fact I absolutely don't want you to, that's not why I showed you, hear me out on this"

"In God's name why not, if anything happens to Carol I couldn't live with myself."

"I'm an experienced journalist and judge of character Bill, I'd stake my life the story is false."

"You're not staking your life though are you, you're staking that young girl's life!"

"Actually she's twenty two I spoke with her and I'm certain she's not in danger, slow down and look at it, you're a human rights lawyer, smell the coffee, these are our friends, OK acquaintances really but we liked them, they liked us, friends in a way and I think they may need help. I think they might be getting set up and that in itself is very interesting, why would someone want them so badly they'd risk framing them in the press?

"For a start there's no detail, nothing at all that can be corroborated. I called a colleague in London, never heard of a serial killer by that name and said the story wasn't running in the UK and nor was it likely to, she said it was embargoed at best and that an injunction may mean it never runs in the UK.

"Now why would that be? Eh, a serial killer in the UK would be major news, fair game, public interest, not quashed. So then I asked why it had been suppressed and the answer, wait for it national security. I ask you a serial killer with vague victims and no detail, happened in the UK, but only running the story in the US. Well?"

"Well, if they know he's here, they'd run it here to protect the public, but I admit it's damned odd."

"It's not just odd, it's fake, they're not after this Mike because he's killed anyone at all, it must be because he knows something they want hushed up, it's the only thing that explains the national security thing in the UK, and two other things whilst were on it, one, get to the bottom of it and it could be the stuff of a Pulitzer Prize, and secondly these are nice people, come on we know it, just one evening alone and a bit of time in company at Sturgis sure, but first impressions are rarely wrong, you and I, we're both very experienced with people we know lies and honesty, these are basically friends who may need a lot of help to get out of some very deep water."

"Did you get a number?"

"No, they took our cards but didn't offer their contact details and I didn't push, I could sense somehow that they wouldn't be forthcoming and now I have a sense of why. I just hope they reach out to us, my goodness I do."

"You know if it comes out we withheld information it could be us in deep water."

"Well, I have a very good lawyer and anyway, trust me I'm a journalist!"

"That's a good one! I love you though and I know when you're onto something. I won't call the cops."

"Promise"

"Promise, I like being married. To you."

"And you'll think about what to ask if they do get in touch and how best to handle it?"

"I'll think of nothing else!"

"Now you're just being silly! Give me a kiss."

The following morning Tanya went for her early morning run before work and reappeared, somewhat breathless, after only a few minutes. She threw down the East Bay Times and The San Francisco Chronicle.

"You need to see these!"

"Why?"

"Not front page thank god, which struck me as strange actually, but look at page five in the Times and page seven in the Chronicle."

"Jesus, Joseph and Mary, you know this isn't true don't you."

"I'm pretty sure it isn't, but now you have to tell me what is true."

"Look there's no detail in these stories, which must be why the editors didn't feel comfortable to make it front page news. It also pretty much answers one question, whether or not Russian agents are after me or not US Law Enforcement are and that means the British are too, because how the hell..."

"Mike, stop, I've grown up these last months I need to know the full story, no omissions, that's what people in a committed relationship do, secrets, titbits, things out of context which mislead, it's, well, it's pretty much the same as lying."

"OK last chance to choose not to know because it might put you in danger too."

"I need to know Mike, we've come this far together, we've both taken risks for each other, we've worked together, shared everything, I have to know and I have to know now, because you or we have to get out of here."

"Me, I think, you have uni to think about a career, a future, if you'll wait for me then somehow I will get out of this mess. OK here it is, it's going to sound pretty far fetched though."

After about forty five minutes of full and honest explanations the questions started.

"So any person who is exposed to this signal just stops functioning?"

"That's about the long and the short of it."

"So drivers crash, maybe pilots too, surgeons, anaesthetist and nurses all just stop in the middle of an operation!"

"Yes, people would die, but compare it with a tactical nuke or the like, far fewer die, enemies are disarmed, taken into custody and anyway there was talk about developments to try and make it more directional, less blanket so to speak. Friendly troops would simply wear receivers and headsets with a sort of antidote wave to cancel the one paralysing the opposition. Far less cumbersome than gas masks and suits.

"I have to say the idea of an army going into battle in their Sony Walkmans did tickle me. I'm reading between the lines now but I think the British invented it, that chap should never have taken it home, let alone have left it in my cab when his wife shouted at him. Someone from another intelligence agency was watching him and it was them who kidnapped me.

"At the time I thought they were Russians, but, I think now that was done to mislead me, the way I see it is that this thing is only of use if the enemy don't have it too. If the Russians have it already, not much point in the CIA or MI6 or anyone else coming after me, especially if it's in the public domain. They don't though do they, that's why the Americans and the British are so keen to get to me, I'm the loose cannon, the guy who's outside their sphere who knows too much and has to be silenced."

"My god Mike, they wouldn't kill you."

"Why not? Nations sacrifice individuals for the greater good as they see it. Can you imagine, the CIA and MI6 together, unable to catch a London Cabby on the run, they must be beside themselves. The missing persons thing that set me running again was bad enough, but this is totally desperate bull crap.

"That's why there's no detail, because anyone checking would find no murders took place, I'll lay odds the story isn't running in the UK either, there would have to have been previous stories and unless they've been planning this step for months there will not be a string of fake murder stories in the British press."

"They're banking on me being spotted and arrested pronto and then the story will disappear. I've got to leave the country, I've still got Dave's passport."

"Well that's no use is it, it'll be cancelled and ports and airports will be notified to look out for someone calling himself Dave Harrison."

"Yes, you're right. You do realise that literally thousands of people saw us together don't you, then there's all the people around here. Maybe I should ask the Angels to shelter me they wouldn't give away a brother."

"You're not a member though are you, just peripheral and anyway it only takes one, if the authorities don't get a quick result there'll be a reward for information next! Hmm university fees!

I'm only kidding"

"I'm glad you can see the funny side it's not your head on the block!"

"It might be now you've told me."

"Oh Jesus I'm sorry."

"Don't be, even if I didn't know it sounds like they might not take the risk. Anyway, you made the joke about marines in Walkmans, I guess we have to try and see the funny side somehow. Josey did the late night shift at the pharmacy, she'll still be in bed for a few hours. I'm going to pop out and get all the papers, see if any of them say anything more or anything different."

Ten minutes later the bed was covered in newspapers, national and local. It was apparent that all the papers carried the story, suspiciously, without the prominence it should really attract given the subject matter. It was also clear that all the articles were short and almost exactly the same, word for word nearly.

Tanya found herself idly looking at classified ads at the back of one of the San Francisco papers, whilst she mulled the problem over in her head.

"I've got it!"

"Got what?"

"Your escape route!"

"Really?"

"Look at this."

At the back of a local paper there was an advertisement from an elderly couple with a yacht, seeking crew for a voyage to Central America at least and maybe beyond, final destination southern Chile.

"You know that might work. If they haven't seen this news I reckon I can sell myself, I don't know anything about sailing, but I know plenty about engines by now and I'm still quite fit and strong."

"You can't be seen, but I know where Josey hides her car keys I'll run you down to the marina, if you can ingratiate yourself quickly and stay on the boat till it leaves that would be good, you're too well known here. If you need picking up I'll see if I can borrow Josey's car legitimately later, or I might have to risk a taxi, but one thing at a time, let's try and get you on that boat, before there's a knock at the door."

"We need a plan for you too. If I take a thousand dollars in cash you'll have a ton of money here still, in the bank and in cash."

"You'll need more than a thousand."

"No, I won't, I can't spend it at sea and the ad says expenses covered. You'll need more than money though, you'll either need to move on which isn't so good given your job and your aim to get into Berkeley, or you'll potentially need legal help. You're American, you have rights here, but neither of us knows the legal system, we know someone who does though. Drop me off at the marina and as soon as you get back call Bill and Charlotte. Then play it by ear as to how much you tell them, they'll help, I'm sure they will, right up their alley."

"What?"

"English expression."

Half an hour later Mike met David and Linda Hayes aboard their thirty six foot sloop Allegria. They took to each other immediately. David and Linda were very experienced sailors, it was just that arthritis and old age were catching up on them and the sloop carried a large mainsail on a tall mast and a very large genoa as well as a smaller storm jib. They were worried about one of them having to handle one or two large sails alone, whilst the other helmed in a sudden squall. Late September was a pretty good time of year to go sailing in the Pacific, but nothing is guaranteed with oceans or weather.

Mike introduced himself as Dave Harrison and had a passport to confirm it.

"Two Daves eh" joked Linda.

"If I'm issuing instructions from the helm you'll have to be Dave two OK?"

"I'm fine with that."

"We'd be really happy to have you along, we've sailed for years, but if we have a weakness it's knowledge of engines so you're perfect for us, the thing is that ad in the paper, it's been running for weeks with no takers, so we'd given up, checked out, leave in an hour. I don't think you'll be able to make arrangements in that time."

"I don't have sailing gear, but I've got shorts, beach shoes, t-shirts, underwear and some cash in that holdall. I travel light, if you have sailing clothes I can get into?"

"Oh yes, we always carry way too much stuff, what about the formalities?"

"I'll take the risk if you will, I'm a bit of a rebel at heart."

"Well then, shake?"

"Shake."

With departure time bearing down David and Linda had had no interest in the media. For them life recently had been all about checking equipment, especially emergency equipment and first aid stuff, fuelling, filling up the fresh water, provisioning, making sure everything that needed charging was charged, checking lines for chaffing, checking the seams in their sails, making passage plans and many other things. They were oblivious to the presence of a supposed serial killer on the loose.

Half an hour after dropping Mike at the harbour Tanya was on the phone to Charlotte and before that conversation had even finished Dave Two was raising the main sail as Dave One unfurled the genoa and Linda set course away from shore, close hauled at six, sometimes seven knots.

"Charlotte?"

"Carol?"

"Yes, well, that's not actually my name, I need your help."

"I know, I saw the press release last night. I've been praying you'd call."

"Really, I'm not in danger from Mike, you do know that."

"Oh yes I smelled a fake instantly, the story that is. I already called contacts in London there aren't any murders, no victims, there aren't stories in the press over there either, but your boyfriend is in some kind of big trouble, someone wants to find him, it's closed down in the UK on national security grounds!

Anyhow, this is desperate stuff. I mean, if, I should say when really, it becomes apparent he never harmed anyone the libel suits, well, the sky's the limit the way things work here."

"Slow down Charlotte, right now I just want him to be free and safe and that goes for me too. Look I can't tell you everything, not right now anyway."

Scenting her Pulitzer Charlotte knew to go gently on Carol, but she also knew she'd have to move fast as well, it was unlikely she'd be the only curious journalist, but she had the advantage, the head start, of knowing the accused and his girlfriend.

"Bill and I will do everything we can to help honey and Bill really knows the law, well you know that, especially a person's rights!"

Bill looked up from his coffee as Charlotte committed them both to leave immediately for San Francisco.

"It's about six hours in the car, depending on traffic in the city we can be with you between four and five pm maybe, give me your address and stay put, we're leaving now."

CHAPTER SIXTEEN - A SMALL WAR IN CENTRAL AMERICA

Guatemala suffered thirty six years of civil war, a war which started in 1960, officially ended in 1996 with a peace accord. Sadly the signing of a peace accord after thirty six years of atrocities, genocide, ethnic cleansing was just the beginning of a new series of obstacles to overcome for that beleaguered nation.

The USA, self declared champions of democracy, had backed a Coup D'etat against the democratically elected left wing government as far back as 1954, presumably feeling that a left wing government on their doorstep was an open door for the Soviets and making a right wing fascist dictatorship, supplied by the USA and assisted by the CIA a much better option for Uncle Sam. So, not that keen on democracy if they didn't like the result apparently.

CIA roots went deep in Guatemala. The peace accord of 1996 largely succeeded in bringing overt conflict to an end, however it also led to criminal gangs calling themselves security services operating alongside the government security service which itself had a far greater impact on society than in nations that had known peace for rather longer and which had more mature apparatus of government and institutions.

The CIA kept a low profile post '96 but it did not go away by any means.

The Xinka are reckoned to be the oldest of the indigenous peoples, from before even the Maya made their appearance in history. Xinka ancestral lands in the south east of Guatemala on the Pacific side stretch up to the northern highlands. Unfortunately for them their lands are good for growing coffee and below the ground are resources such as gold, silver, lead and zinc.

Attacks on Xinka populations and their leaders and attacks on their lands by commercial interests did not end in 1996 they just became slightly more subtle. It became slightly less apparent who was pulling the strings, mining companies, criminal 'security' organisations, government security, the CIA or combinations of all of the above. Xinka leaders were perplexed and tragically were periodically assassinated. It was a war in all but name.

Julio Luis Gonzalez sat in a bar in the city of Naranjo near the Naranjo River. He was with a group of comrades and he was hearing strange tales about his people in the remote villages collapsing, waking up miles away from home, unsure where they were, unable to remember what had happened to them, or how to get back.

Was there some kind of epidemic? Common sense suggested not, people who collapse with illness don't always recover and even those who do are unlikely to have walked two hundred miles or more in a trance. It was inexplicable, but, given the thirty six years war had finished less than five years ago, with all the massacres, the still latent hatred, genocides, villages wiped out and subsequent jostling for power and natural resources, foul play was the entirely logical and really the only reasonable conclusion.

How it was being done, why it was being done, these were the questions he and his village elders and comrades needed answering and not a one had any real idea. Of course there were broad brush theories about the why aspect. It's about fruit, or coffee, or gold, silver, lead, zinc, some large commercial organisation was always waiting in the wings to rape the natural resources of Central America and suspicion naturally fell, and with good reason, on the large, powerful neighbour to the north, who'd sponsored the coup in the 1950s that had pushed Guatamala down this long, bloody and tragic road.

"We should split up, do some travelling, ask questions, but be careful, trust no one, the American Government has killed before, big business will do the same and that's before we even look at the criminal gangs who may want control of the resources our land has, our land comrades and it's not on offer. The fight continues. I will go south to the coast and keep my ear to the ground, that's where there are the most comings and goings of people and equipment, we also need to have ears at the airport and in all the major towns. We'll divide responsibilities, actually, I think there are enough of us at this meeting that we can work in pairs, watch each other's backs.

"Let's decide on the pairs and who will go where, then meet up back here in two weeks. Don't trust telephones, don't write anything down, two weeks right here, same time, we share whatever we find out. Don't get yourselves killed."

Julio paired up with his son Gabor and headed south for the coast.

CHAPTER SEVENTEEN - THE WINDS OF CHANGE

Sailing with David and Linda was a joy which helped compensate a little for the achy, breaky heart that was troubling Mike. He soon discovered that Linda was an excellent cook and knew how to create great tasting dishes from seemingly boring ingredients with a long shelf life such as beans, lentils, dried milk, herbs, some dried and some which she grew on board, eggs which she had coated in wax to preserve them and that was after all the fresh fruit and veg had been used up. They were well stocked with tinned provisions too. The labels had been removed so they wouldn't fall off and turn to mush if they got wet in the bilges, that sort of thing could risk clogging the bilge pumps, however the contents of each tin had been written on in indelible marker.

There was even fresh bread from sealed plastic packets of part baked baguettes which, being part baked already didn't use too much precious gas and filled the boat with the homely smell of fresh bread. Mike was amazed to find there was also fresh ground, real coffee; coffee beans kept well in sealed packets, a hand grinder needed no power and there was plenty of time, one of those little Italian, aluminium devices with a pot on top and a water reservoir at the bottom could sit on the hob and make real espresso!

In bad weather hot water could still be produced in a wide kettle on the hob atop the gimballed cooker, David and Linda had huge mugs, which were only ever half filled to prevent spillages, but which could be used for instant soup as well as tea, or, in a storm, instant coffee or hot chocolate. Mike lamented the lack of cocoa, but really he felt spoilt.

Cup-a-soup might not be the healthy option but in bad weather it made you feel you'd had something substantial, especially if it had lumps of reconstituted vegetables or croutons. Likewise couscous only needed boiling water and shortly afterwards you had something more solid than soup which could be flavoured with olives, fish, herbs and other ingredients from jars or tins. It too could be eaten from mugs with just a spoon and there were strategically positioned mug holders all around, which could be folded flat when not in use.

Mike had developed an enquiring mind about just about anything and everything as a cabby, he was keen to learn all there was to know about living on a boat and travelling on one. He thought, not without reason, that such skills might be handy one day for someone living off grid! He was amazed to find out just how much storage there was on a relatively small yacht. David had made a sketch of the boat with every single storage space given a letter. Fortuitously there were twenty six spaces, under the bunks under the seating, in the bilges, built in cupboards and wardrobes, cockpit lockers and so on.

This A to Z sketch had been laminated to protect it from damp and it had a companion laminate which listed the contents of each location. As a result, if memory failed, tools, filters, clothes, bin bags, fishing gear, lubricants, gasket materials, particular food stuffs, diving goggles and fins, books, instruction manuals, spare parts, distilled water, first aid items, back up radios, light bulbs, fuses, you name it, even if it was needed very infrequently that item, whatever it was, could be located almost instantly without turning the boat into a crime scene.

Looking at the list Mike enquired why they might need bolt cutters and a crow bar.

"Things weigh less under water, when I was younger I could free dive to ten metres and stay there a surprisingly long time. If an anchor became trapped I never had to abandon it, hence the crow bar, not sure I could do it now, but I bet you could!

"The crow bar and the bolt cutters have another use too. In port we always try to steal a couple of push bikes to get around while we're there."

"What!"

"I'm kidding Dave, if a stay or a shroud breaks the mast could come down, complete with sail and boom and drag in the water. They're not likely to break in calm weather so if the mast goes over the side it could turn us over before you know it, the bolt cutters enable us to abandon it as fast as possible and some bits may need levering overboard so the crow bar might come in handy in that emergency too."

"You seem to have thought of everything."

"It's impossible to think of everything, but we have experience and we plan ahead, there's no triple A auto breakdown assistance in the middle of the ocean, a rescue can take hours or even days, best to be prepared, there are sharp knives mounted in handy places to cut running rigging if something is jammed and needs to go, there are flares and grab bags."

"What's a grab bag?"

"A grab bag is something you grab as you step up into the life raft it contains food, flares, things to repair the life raft and a pump to keep it pumped up. Actually we have several grab bags with more in them than most people. We carry a six man life raft which can be a bit light with only two or three people in it, but we have three large plastic, water tight grab bags so we include treats like chocolate for morale, as well as dried fruits and nuts for sustenance, we have a charged hand held radio in there, as well as flares and a charged hand held GPS, and if that runs down we at least have a hand held compass, also binoculars and a night sight, an EPIRB, a search and rescue transponder and a lightweight carbon pole to raise it up.

"If Allegria went down we'd try to salvage the dinghy too, it has sails and could tow the life raft albeit slowly, which would then be our survival cell for sleeping and shade. We carry a lot of things in our grab bags, but we don't have a satellite phone, nor is there an SSB radio on the yacht, partly because we like the solitude and don't want to be tempted to call people.

In any case the EPIRB should do the trick in an emergency. We also have several, part filled, large water containers; fresh water, or the lack thereof will kill you pretty quickly, far more quickly than a lack of food and in addition we have a solar still to get fresh water from seawater, but that's fragile and very slow, however it's belts and braces and it folds up small so it is easy to include in a grab bag."

"Wow, a lot to take in but three immediate questions from all that. Why did you say step up into the life raft, not down, what's an EPIRB and why are the water containers not full given water is so precious?"

Dave explained about how the yacht has supplies, tools, clothes and loads more you cannot fit into a grab bag. You don't abandon ship until it's awash and completely, definitely going down, therefore you step up into the life raft not down from the deck, if you have to step down you've given up too soon!

An EPIRB is an electronic position indicating radio beacon. It sends a distress message to a satellite which transmits the position to a listening station in the northern or southern hemisphere as appropriate. The EPIRB is registered so that the name and type of boat and likely number of occupants are known and the nearest search and rescue or other shipping can be asked to assist and they will know the position and what they're looking for.

Finally grab bags and especially water containers have to be sealed with enough air to ensure they float, a sinking is a fraught emergency, usually, although not always, in rough water, toss something into the life raft and miss, you want it to float in case you get the chance to salvage it.

In the calm evenings Mike found himself having long chats with Dave, he learned how dangerous the cooking gas is on a small boat, a gas explosion could destroy the boat instantly, hence gas alarms as well as bilge water alarms. The cooking gas is heavier than air, if it leaks it can build up in the bilges until, flick an electrical switch and boom, no more boat, no more people. Gas lockers should drain overboard but some older boats weren't designed with that in mind and drains can become blocked if not checked.

At night Dave and Linda normally reduced sail and just meandered along. They were in no particular hurry and reducing sail in a sudden squall is much easier in daylight. The idea was that the night watches would be three hours on six off with two people sleeping but Mike was used to being awake and working long night hours in his cab even if he'd not done it for a long time. He quite often extended his watch to keep Dave or Linda company and to learn all he could from them.

Despite having no formal qualification or training he was fast becoming an expert yachtsman. He understood a bit about first aid and sea survival now, what medication to carry, Dave and Linda even had dental kits so they could work on each other's teeth if it came to it. Mike understood the points of sail, reefing down, tacking, gybing, planning waypoints, navigation, how to interpret a radar screen, radio procedures, such as call signs, Pan Pans and Maydays and what the difference was, also the fact that you never ever say 'over and out', it's one or the other because it's a contradiction, 'over' means you require a response, 'out' means you don't, conversation over in fact! Hollywood eh. Yanks! Then he remembered he was in love with a Yank and very fond of the two wonderful people he was travelling with.

Given there was no need for extra water or provisions, the weather was wonderful, the sailing fun and the company good the three happy sailors just continued cruising south, they were out of American waters not so very far from El Salvador when trouble struck.

'If marine parts were made to the same standards as aircraft parts, which they aren't, then this would never have happened!' thought Dave one.

It was morning and Mike, that is Dave two, was hoisting the mainsail, overnight they'd been ghosting along on a part reefed foresail alone, had Dave one been doing the job he'd have realised the resistance was too great, but Mike had been delegated the more physical jobs and he'd just assumed this level of resistance to be normal. In fact the masthead pulley had deteriorated with sun and age and the wheel component had started breaking up and the halyard, the rope that hoists the sail had been chafing. Suddenly the halyard broke and the mainsail fell back.

With the halyard running inside the hollow aluminium mast, changing it at sea wasn't simple. Dave and Linda carried copious spares, so they had shackles and pulleys and the right length and gauge of rope to replace the halyard. They also had a bosun's chair to winch someone to the top of the mast, but this would normally be done using the halyard! With Dave being a belts and braces kinda guy there were also fold out steps on the mast so it could be climbed, but a safety line wasn't easy to jury rig with the halyard gone and clipping on wasn't possible every step of the way.

Still, the sea was calm and Mike was game, he donned a safety harness, attached a safety line to clip on with where possible, such as at the spreaders or where there were brackets for mast mounted items and tied one end of the new halyard to the tool belt Dave had given him to wear, although he only took a small screwdriver which would pass through the hole on the shackle pin so it could be done up tight and the new pulley, with shackle attached went into another compartment on his belt.

They continued sailing under the foresail, the motion of the boat actually being more gentle and predictable whilst sailing than it would have been just bobbing around in the swell. Mike was agile and although careful, it didn't take many minutes before he was three quarters of the way up the very tall mast. Bermudan sloops, as they are known, tend to have taller masts than ketches or yawls which have two masts and a greater array of sails. Ordinarily a sloop such as Allegria relied on just the main and foresail, so for speed and to achieve the desired sail area, masts tend to be tall enough to carry a large mainsail.

At the three quarter mark then, where the second set of spreaders extended from the mast, Mike looked down, primarily to make sure Dave wasn't trying to give him instructions and to see that the new halyard trailing behind him wasn't getting caught up. There was no problem on that score, Dave was paying it out gently so there was no excess flapping around. Mike had neglected the opportunity to clip on, although spreaders were never designed to take the weight of a human being anyway.

What shook Dave however was just how tiny Allegria looked from up here, looking down from the mast certainly gave an entirely different perspective compared with looking up and he still had the last quarter to climb. He also registered that the higher he went the greater the arc he travelled as the boat rocked, even though at deck level it appeared to be barely rocking at all.

At that moment several things happened more or less simultaneously, the boat suddenly heeled, sped up and pulled around as a sudden, strong gust of wind took a hold of the jib. Mike suddenly found himself clinging on for dear life, his heart pounding as the view below him switched from white decks to blue ocean. At the same moment Linda arrived topside from the cabin and yelled, "the pressure is plummeting".

"Dave ordered Mike to retrace his steps and come down slowly and carefully."

Mike didn't need telling twice, but had the sense to do it very slowly and with great precision as to where he put his hands and feet, making sure to move only one thing at a time. As he got lower the arc became less although in fact the motion was less of a problem than the angle. Dave didn't want to reduce the size of the jib whilst Mike was still coming down, so Allegria was heeled over and travelling at a fair rate of knots. As soon as Mike was on deck and clipped on Dave rolled some of the jib away.

"I'll make you some tea Mike, you English like tea at times like these don't you!" Linda teased.

He accepted gratefully though and started to skein the spare halyard to go back into its appropriate place as listed on the laminate and returned the tool belt with screwdriver and pulley to Dave for the same reason.

Dave was soon looking at the chart plotter and announced the intention to sail, or motor-sail if necessary to hold the course to a certain Marina Pez Vela at the port of San Jose, near the town of Puerto Quetzal.

Most of the boats in the marina would turn out to be what are known as big-game fishing boats, or offshore sport fishing boats, but Allegria could get in there and with everything from cargo ships to cruise ships stopping nearby there would be plenty of services.

"Actually" Dave said "There aren't so many places to stop in Guatemala, not on the Pacific side anyway, more on the Atlantic coast but we should be able to get there by dark and looking at the way the pressure is dropping the sooner the better, I don't know if it's a small storm coming, or a full blown cyclone, they do occur in this region and the cyclone season isn't really over for a few more weeks.

"We can't continue the voyage without a mainsail either, well, we could but it's far from ideal and I don't like problems piling up, so that's it, we're going to Guatemala folks and we'll stay until Allegria is fixed. We can avoid the storm, looks like a pretty safe harbour and we can refill the potable water tanks and get fresh food too!"

Mike wasn't unhappy with this, it wasn't the USA, but could he avoid showing his passport, would all points of entry everywhere be looking for him, did Guatemala have an extradition treaty with the USA? He had no answer to any of these conundrums, nor did he want to drag Dave and Linda into his problems. He pretty much felt he'd be best jumping ship at this point but no need to make that decision yet, he'd be just as happy to sail to Ecuador, Peru, Chile, all on Dave and Linda's agenda but at every new country the passport could give him away should he need to show it, if he could make it through this time why risk it again?

He decided to forewarn Dave and Linda that he was at least contemplating staying in Guatemala so that if he did make that decision they'd be prepared.

By the time they arrived Mike was decided, he had a chat with Dave and Linda and tried to make a fishy story sound plausible. He reminded them he hadn't checked out of the USA and said he didn't know if that would cause a problem checking in here. He said he fancied spending some time in Guatemala and that he'd have his bag ready and if there was a chance to slip away that was what he intended to do. He didn't want to make life difficult for them but if he hopped ashore and vanished it might be as well to say it was just the two of them, rather than trying to explain a missing crew member.

Dave and Linda seemed a little perplexed, but said it was his call, they'd fly the customs flag to show they weren't officially in the country but if there was an opportunity for him to step off unseen, they wouldn't risk upsetting the authorities.

In the event, as so often happens when sailing the planned arrival in daylight didn't occur as the seas became ever more choppy and progress even under motor slowed. With Dave and Linda's assistance and blessing Mike was able to hop ashore in the dark on to one pontoon before they continued to another and dutifully stayed aboard until the authorities could check them out.

Mike made good his escape and found his way into the city of Puerto Quetzal where he was just one amongst thousands of people. That was as far as his planning really took him, but a commercial port like that meant a plethora of languages, mostly Spanish, but plenty of English too. His first step was to find a bar with a television. That way he might see the news, and at the same time hear some local gossip, which in and of itself might lead to a plan, or even, if he was very lucky, a place to stay. After all, it happened once before.

Spanish was de-facto a second language in the USA, you couldn't spend the amount of time state-side that Mike had without picking up a few words. The television news when it came on held no terrors, nothing about a missing man, no names associated with him and no pictures of a serial killer.

Mike, Dave and Linda had sailed approximately three thousand nautical miles, with no urgency, they had often sailed at a mere three knots at night time, five knots in daylight apart from the occasional calm, Mike realised, having not really tallied up before that it was now late October. The serial killer story had become yesterday's news, even in the USA where it had been impossible to feed the media any new developments, given there were none and it wasn't possible to feed the news more fake stories given that sooner or later some journalist or other would look into it.

However something in the bar was causing agitation amongst the locals. An older man and someone who could be a son, nephew, or much younger brother were asking questions. In fact the strange goings on in Xinka lands wasn't the best kept secret anyway, it had spawned gossip and gossip travels. Under these circumstances Julio and Gabor felt they didn't need to keep such a low profile after all. They were almost openly asking what people knew, after all they weren't the only ones to find the stories perplexing.

Again and again Mike heard words he could work out even if he didn't know them, words like personas, colapser, coma, perdida de memoria. Others like enfermedad and secuestrar he had picked up in the USA anyway. It was a picture that suggested people were collapsing and being kidnapped and losing their memories. 'My god, someone is using it' he thought, and I'm here, the only person outside the security services who knows what the hell it is. He actually wondered if life was pre-ordained and if the decisions we make are entirely meaningless.

Mike approached the elder man.

"Hable Ingles?"

He thought that might not be the full expression but perhaps he'd be understood.

"No, pero mi hijo si, Gabor ven aqui."

"What exactly are you asking about, because I think I may know something that might help you."

Gabor started to explain and very, very quickly Mike stops him and whispers.

"Yes, I know what this is and this knowledge has been very dangerous for me, people are looking for me. I think I can help your people, can you get me to a safe place where we can talk properly?"

CHAPTER EIGHTEEN - THE MAKING OF TANYA

After assuring Josey that Mike was in no way violent, let alone a killer, let alone a multiple killer and making her swear secrecy, Monkey had turned up at the door. After reassuring him and pointing out the problems with the whole story a second time Bill and Charlotte had arrived. Tanya was exhausted, it was mental exhaustion and stress more than physical exhaustion, but no less debilitating for that.

"Oh Charlotte, Bill, I'm so glad you're here, it's been the day from hell, I'm exhausted and scared of making bad choices."

Charlotte made a snap decision, which although Bill rolled his eyes he couldn't really fault.

"OK sweetheart, why don't you grab your things and come with us back to LA. If anyone from around here recognises Mike, they'll put him together with you and before you know it they'll be knocking on the door or hanging around the neighbourhood. Back home we can feed you, you can sleep in peace, no one will find you and you can tell us as much or as little as you want, when you want.

"We know it's all fake, but Mike must be in big trouble, the Feds wouldn't go to so much trouble or take the risk"

"We don't think it's the FBI, we think it's the CIA and MI6."

Charlotte took a deep breath. "Wow."

"Get your things, we're getting you out of here lady, when we get you home you can have a relaxing herbal bath, something to eat and drink if you want and you can sleep safe as you like, for as long as you need. Then we'll take stock of the situation and see what can be done."

Tanya packed a couple of bags, she had to use shopping bags, Mike had her holdall, she left a note for Josey saying she intended to lie low a while but she'd like to keep the room on and she'd be in touch, she telephoned work to say she was sick but would be back in as soon as she could and climbed into Bill's car for the drive back to LA.

It was three o'clock the following afternoon when Tanya awoke, four by the time she'd showered, dressed and made an appearance in the living room where she found Charlotte anxiously waiting for her.

"Where's Bill?"

"He's having a meeting with a new client, well the guy isn't the client, it'll be one of the NGOs or charities; Bill does work for many of them NAACP, Children's Defense Fund, Amnesty, Human Rights Action Center. It's a twenty something from Guatemala I think, but it's you I'm worried about.

"Don't tell me anything that makes you uncomfortable and start at the beginning, do you mind if I record our conversation, it can be hard to remember everything, even with notes."

"I guess not, but can we wait for Bill, I'd rather he heard it first hand, I'd rather not do it all twice and I think I'm going to need a good lawyer."

Charlotte agreed, opened a couple of beers and they waited for Bill to come in. It wasn't a long wait, at five thirty came the sound of Bill's key in the lock, followed by "Hello ladies, you have one of those for me?"

Tanya started at the very beginning and told the entire story of her personal circumstances at home, leading to her running away through to meeting Mike on the highway, travelling together, getting the bike, of course they knew about Sturgis but she filled them in on why she and Mike had travelled to San Francisco, how they'd found a place to stay and a way to make money. She realised in the telling how strange it must sound and yet Bill and Charlotte showed no sign of doubt or cynicism, purely concern.

Tanya hesitated a bit when it came to details about how Mike had got away again, but decided she needed to tell them, she asked if they could keep it to themselves.

"You know if I'm your lawyer I have to treat everything as confidential, you do also know however, that my dear wife is a journalist don't you" at which point he shot Charlotte a questioning look.

"OK I can offer two promises if you're happy to share more, one I won't publish anything, not a single word without your permission and two we all have to make sure Mike is safe and try to extricate him from whatever he's caught up in before we even decide if we can go public and whether going public helps, and I have never given those kinds of assurances before, but I suspect there's more going on here than just the story, I think there may be a monumental injustice and that man there would not have married a journo if we didn't share the same moral compass!"

Mike had told Tanya almost everything he knew, he'd been a bit light on detail about how the tech worked, but had told her about it incapacitating people and so on and of course that it involved some kind of transmitter and a head set system worn to prevent ill effects on the users' own personnel.

Tanya told the story, largely verbatim as she had heard it from Mike, of the computer in the taxi, how Mike's curiosity had gotten the better of him, how the passenger's wife's verbal attack on her husband had accidentally tipped Mike off and given him the key to defeating the password. She explained about the kidnap, the escape and why Mike had felt the need to flee and how he'd achieved it. She told Bill and Charlotte how Mike had hid out with Sarah in the trailer and how they too got by financially, leading to Sarah gifting Mike the truck he'd been driving when he'd come across Tanya.

Tanya explained how, eventually, as events unfolded, they'd realised there were no Russians and that they'd reached the conclusion that it must have been the CIA duping him and that they must have teamed up with British Military Intelligence, probably, only after Mike had eluded them.

Charlotte did not yet have a digital recorder and had changed tapes about ten times, all carefully numbered for continuity when they realised it was now ten o'clock in the evening and all they'd consumed was beer. They ordered a Chinese delivery, took more beers out of the refrigerator and agreed to discuss all the implications tomorrow, after a good night's sleep.

The following morning Bill took the lead in the discussions over breakfast, Charlotte called a friend and asked her to call round with another twenty tapes for her voice recorder and cancelled the cleaner, no one must know they had a house guest.

Bill expressed the view that the first thing that needed doing was to write to every paper that had published the serial killer story with the threat of legal action. He said that whilst there was no budget to take legal action he could write to them in legal speak on his headed paper and that the threat alone would almost certainly kill the story dead.

On the downside, his doing that would alert the security services; his involvement in writing to the media would make no sense whatsoever unless he was involved with Mike in some way. However they wouldn't risk kidnapping a famous human rights lawyer married to a journalist and they certainly wouldn't take them both in. He might face some official questioning, although he doubted they'd want to make an issue of it and if they did he could always fall back on lawyer, client confidentiality.

What they would do is to put him and Charlotte under surveillance. The good thing about that is that it would be a waste of their time, but Tanya would have to be gone from their home by the time the letters went out in order to remain out of the picture where the security services were concerned.

That too was good, she could return to Josey's place, return to her job, make her application to Berkeley, get on with her life basically. He would consider asking the papers to print an apology and state that the photo was of the wrong person, but he wasn't sure if that was going too far, it would strongly suggest Mike was his client. What did the others think.

Charlotte suggested that a retraction like that would take any remaining heat off Tanya, journalists would lose interest in the story once it was clearly erroneous at best, but this way any individual who'd seen Tanya with Mike would realise there was nothing to be gained from trying to find her, or turn them in so to speak. If only one or two papers even apologised for printing the wrong picture it would get around and other papers would likely follow suit.

"Besides" she said "We're used to taking these kinds of risks, Tanya is not, nor does she have backing from the legal establishment or the media, we do."

Bill said he'd do his best, but that he wanted to know more about this bizarre weapon before he went back to the office, he'd agreed to help the scared young man from Guatemala, but he didn't yet know the ins and outs of the case and there was to be a meeting with Amnesty and the client as he was known in about ninety minutes, meaning he had half an hour before he had to leave.

Tanya explained that the weapon was a way to disable people without killing them, that they could then be disarmed and that it would disorient them for a while afterwards. She claimed not to know how it worked, so there was no mention of transmitters or headsets and conversation moved on to when Tanya should call work and Josey and get back to San Francisco.

Bill undertook, despite today's briefing, to write the letter that day. An assistant would research and check which media had run the story and he promised that the letters would reach all the editors the next day by courier, the expense of which would be a contribution from him.

In order to not risk her job, or her tenure of the room in Josey's house, Tanya would need to call work and Josey that day. Charlotte could do the driving this time and he suggested they went late that night or early the following morning to avoid the worst of the traffic and to get Tanya back to work before questions were asked or her position at the hotel put at risk.

Charlotte appeared disappointed, she'd hoped to share her home with Tanya in the knowledge that extra bits of information would inevitably slip out, or get confided, over time, but she agreed that getting Tanya's life on track was the most important thing. She also said she'd find ways to be in touch and to set up a way that Tanya could reach out to them without the CIA knowing, burner phones, intermediaries, whatever, the paper knew how to do these things, so did Amnesty come to that, communication would reopen, they'd contact her; anyone genuine but unknown to Tanya would open the conversation by asking how Tanya had enjoyed the Cher concert at Sturgis. An innocent enough question and it would suggest to anyone overhearing that they already knew each other.

As if it had all been a dream, Tanya found herself back living with Josey and back at her job, the cash reserves would feed and house her for months if not years and her salary and the donations from Mom continued to build up in the various bank accounts. She was anonymous again just like that.

Bill's letters had the desired effect, she occasionally socialised with Josey and Monkey. She politely declined to date HA members and Monkey became almost father like towards her. It occurred to her that HA members could maybe take messages to Bill; as well off financially as the HA were they might be thought of as an oppressed minority who'd taken on a human rights lawyer, no connection to Mike's case whatsoever, nothing anyone would link up.

Mike's story, the fact that she missed him terribly and the way governments pushed the little people around whenever and however they wanted to had awoken a passion for politics in Tanya, something that no one back home could ever have imagined. Actually she couldn't have imagined it herself; mixing with so many different kinds of people, from lawyers and journalists to Hells Angels and bikers had given her an entirely new perspective on people, life, the world.

She read the newspapers now and there were always plenty of papers at work, she watched the news channels, she read political books and summoned up the courage to take evening classes. Now that she was no longer a receptionist but rather head of conferencing her late nights at work were far less frequent if not actually eliminated.

On the basis that one should know ones enemies Tanya read books on the history and activities of both the CIA and MI6, she read about the adventures of her government, Mexico, the Spanish War, Cuba and the Bay of Pigs, Guatemala.

Her application to study politics at Berkeley went without a hitch. Tanya was on her way.

CHAPTER NINETEEN - A QUESTION OF CONSCIENCE

Amnesty International introduced Bill to his new client Felipe from Guatemala. Now twenty two Felipe had made money running errands and carrying messages between the CIA and organisations they backed when he was a young, and even younger looking, teenager. He'd been able to move around without arousing suspicion, he'd been useful.

His contact with the CIA and its methods and attitudes had gradually filled him with loathing for the American government and their security apparatus, not to mention the powerful American businesses which wished only to exploit his country. Felipe was smart though, he never let his feelings show, kept in with his handlers and now that the war was officially over, and operations had moved into a new phase, one of those handlers had assisted Felipe in obtaining a US passport. He now had the right to live and work in the US and to study, which was the reason Felipe had given for wanting to go to the country he had previously served.

In fact what motivated Felipe, a Xinka by heritage, was the strange goings-on in the remote villages which had affected his extended family. He personally would not be taken seriously as a whistle blower, but there were human rights organisations and NGOs who might believe him and who might help. They were generally to the north, in the USA, 'no country is all bad I guess' he thought.

Felipe had been paid for his work and could pay his way in the short term. He managed to get a meeting with Amnesty International who actually, also solved his immediate accommodation problems. Amnesty had appointed a lawyer to the case, one William Standing.

Bill, as everyone knew him, took an immediate interest, almost as if he already had an interest in fact, something which amazed Felipe, but he put it down to the lawyer trying to make him as the client feel relaxed.

That the lawyer then invited him to share his home and meet his wife, a rising star in journalism baffled Felipe but he felt somehow this was what he was meant to do and he gratefully accepted. The Amnesty staff were a little taken aback too and at the end of the meeting took Bill to one side and privately informed him that this special level of service did not warrant a special level of billing! Bill assured them he knew that, and that he knew what he was doing. He'd do some digging and report back.

Bill called Charlotte and warned her they'd be having another house guest almost immediately. Things were moving fast Tanya was there right now, but she'd be leaving late that night, Bill told Felipe he could present himself at their address the following day, he didn't want the two to meet, not yet anyway, but he felt pretty certain that Mike's weapon, as he thought of it, was being trialled on innocent people in remote forests in Central America for the benefit of US corporations and his hackles were up. This was something he could get his teeth into.

The more Bill investigated the history of US intervention, manipulation actually, in Guatemala the more angry Bill became, but he knew better than to become emotional, having the facts at your fingertips, having a good analytical mind, knowing the law and past precedents, knowing how to present a case, these were the things, which in his experience, led to good outcomes.

Bill became certain that Mike's weapon was being trialled in Guatemala, he didn't know if it was just a test, or whether the US government was involved in ethnic cleansing in order to open the way for metal extraction or the like on tribal lands. Either way he considered it despicable.

He guessed it was the former, since there was no evidence of resettlement camps or anything like that and Xinka elders were making strenuous efforts to get people home again. At this point there didn't appear to be any fatalities. Although a couple of elderly people had passed away, cause and effect couldn't be investigated, let alone proven, Old people die.

The CIA were not above acting without orders, but a programme of ethnic cleansing for commercial reasons surely couldn't be put into effect without government sanction. Nothing like that had been publicly debated, there were no announcements of new mines, or increased commercial activity regarding fruit or coffee growing either.

Bill had other clients too, making enquiries, whilst fighting other battles took time, a lot of time. Felipe got a job at McDonalds and bided his time until Bill was ready to report to Amnesty and discuss what actions should, or might be taken. Felipe didn't like just waiting whilst his people suffered, but he'd received a level of support quite unexpected and beyond his means to pay for so he hid his frustrations and waited.

Charlotte had opened up a secure means of communication with Tanya and had asked her to please get in touch if anything was heard from Mike. She advised Tanya that they believed Mike's weapon was being trialled in Guatemala. Two months passed with no news from Mike whilst at the end of that time Bill prepared to report his findings to Amnesty. Before the meeting Bill advised Felipe that he believed the CIA had been trialling a new weapon. However, he said, he must protect his source whose life would be in danger. He warned Felipe not to expect too much from the meeting and assured him that "this is ongoing, and certainly not finished with".

Bill explained his findings to Amnesty and again stated that legal action is not possible without proof, or far stronger evidence and that he could not reveal his source for the sake of that person's safety. What he proposed was that Amnesty try to contact as many Guatemalans living in the USA as possible to protest at the Guatemalan embassy that Xinka people are being oppressed. This will shine a spotlight on the region, possibly cause the CIA to stop what he believes they are doing and if there is government involvement then whatever and whoever in government is involved may have to rethink.

It doesn't bring people to justice, it doesn't expose the entire story, but it may end the misery for now at least. The protest is quite small but Tanya attends with some of her friends from her politics evening group. She's exchanged messages with Bill and Charlotte. She briefly makes eye contact with Bill and Charlotte, but nothing more. American security services take photographs of every face at the demonstration for the files. Potential troublemakers, even the home grown ones.

Tanya called Charlotte on one of the burner phones.

"I know it was risky being there, but I had to do something to help, for Mike, it's a question of conscience that I don't sit around and do nothing."

CHAPTER TWENTY - BEAR TRAPS

Upon meeting Mike, Julio and Gabor realised instantly that they'd stumbled on something more than just the gossip and speculation they'd been hearing for days. They invited him back to their lodgings and jumped in a cab, the rain rattled on the roof and the wind blew hard. Mike was glad David and Linda were tucked up in port behind that enormous break water.

Back at the small house where Julio had begged a room from an old friend there were two single beds, Gabor offered to give his up and sleep on the floor, citing age. Mike wasn't sure whether to be grateful or incensed at the implication that he wasn't young enough, or tough enough, to sleep on the floor.

"I think the Americans are testing a new weapon on your people, but before I tell you what I know you'd better tell me everything that's happened, if after that it still tallies with what I know I believe I will be able to fill in a lot of the blanks for you."

It was a long evening, they conversed slowly with Gabor making the translations, he'd learned English at school, but he'd never had to use it with a native speaker and then there was the accent. Both parties recognised the potential for misunderstandings and so both parties tried to express everything in two different ways.

At the end of the conversation, around three o'clock in the morning Mike pleaded exhaustion, he'd been at sea all day then jumped ship so to speak and then all this, he was dead on his feet. They'd covered a huge amount of ground however and pretty much confirmed the suspicions of both parties.

It was agreed that Mike would accompany Julio and Gabor to Naranjo to meet the other elders, village leaders and volunteers Julio had gathered around himself. Many of whom had experience from the thirty six years war which might prove useful, as might the weapons.

At the end of the war, when the fighting factions agreed a peace, weapons had been surrendered and the weapons surrendered correlated pretty much to the number of fighters, but as for reserve arms cashes and weapons dumps, they stayed hidden as an insurance against hostilities breaking out anew.

Julio had access to plenty of conventional weapons if he needed them, but he didn't want to be the trigger, or spark that re-ignited the war and anyway it sounded as if conventional weapons would be of no use in this scenario. He'd liberate a small number of hand guns that could be used to threaten anyone captured but the automatic rifles and mortars could stay where they were.

Mike attended the meeting in the corner of the otherwise deserted bar in Naranjo, anyone not involved had been invited, in unmistakable tones, by the owner to drink there another day. Gabor did his best to relate Mike's story as accurately as possible and as briefly as possible although many questions ensued and the participants looked at Mike with a mixture of awe, wonderment and suspicion.

It was decided to watch any and all places where Americans hung out, American businesses, basically.

The two Green Berets with a group of local, non Xinka helpers, had been enjoying themselves. It was too easy really. By now the headphones had been incorporated in combat helmets, with a wire inside the tunic to a battery pack at the waist with a simple on off switch, on made you impervious to the transmission, off left you exposed.

The transmitter had been miniaturised, well, in truth the US and British militaries now had a range of transmitters, big powerful, generator powered units on trucks down to the handheld units the Green Berets had been using. They were largely directional and trigger operated, light weight too.

You simply approached the village you wanted to clear, switched your helmet on and pulled the trigger. Within minutes no one was any kind of a threat. A lock on the trigger meant you could keep them that way whilst you loaded them into a truck and sent them on their way. You had to stay with them and keep your helmet turned on in order that they didn't come round too quickly or see something they might possibly remember, but basically it was child's play and no one amongst the guinea pigs had remembered a thing.

Doug and Bruce would be sorry when the exercise came to an end. However, because it had been such a simple, no risk job, as they saw it, they had become sloppy. Julio's people saw them go out on a job, saw them return from that job, heard, naturally that a village had been attacked that day and correctly put the picture together.

Mike and Julio hatched a plan of their own.

"We do not want to kill anyone" Mike said.

"We need to capture them and relieve them of their equipment, that way we have bargaining power, we could even give them a taste of their own medicine, they might have difficulty explaining that to their bosses!"

Julio's people would lay traps on the paths that led from the base unit the Green Berets were using. Bear traps, being the kind of thing where there's a net under the leaves and undergrowth which when someone steps into the middle is powered into the air by a bent tree, and at the same time a drawstring closes over the occupants' heads.

"That's great as far as it goes, but these guys will carry knives which means they operate their device, then while we're incapacitated, they cut their way out and capture us instead of the other way around."

"Yes" said Julio we have to be quicker than they are. "Cuatro pistolas" he said opening a small sack and laying the well oiled weapons on the table, "Touch that thing we all shoot you, you gonna risk it punk?"

They laughed, but there was also tension.

The plan worked though. Warning shots had to be fired and Mike had to shout a verbal warning in English indicating that if they so much as touched the equipment they carried they'd be shot out of hand by four people at once. Mike's English accent was a giveaway. Realising that this would incriminate him it actually became imperative to helmet up and try the device on Doug and Bruce themselves, but before they risked them losing too much memory it was time to interrogate them.

Not being prepared to use torture they got nothing but names and numbers and they came from the dog tags anyway, the Green Berets had been lax but they were no pushover. As well as two helmets for themselves Doug and Bruce carried four more for the helpers they'd expected to rendezvous with, the local helpers were not permitted to keep them between jobs.

Mike and Julio ended up with six helmets and one transmitter, potentially useful one day but beyond testing it out there was no immediate need, the kit would ultimately be carefully wrapped and join the hidden weapons cache against future need.

Bruce and Doug were transported to a remote spot, deep in the forest where they were tied to trees. Mike and Gabor stayed nearby, helmets on their heads and with walkie talkies to communicate with Julio and three others. The four with the transmitter would withdraw approximately half a mile then radio Mike and Gabor to turn their helmet devices on. After that they too would turn their helmets on and, pointing the transmitter in the general direction of the prisoners they would activate it.

Mike and Gabor were to radio back and confirm whether or not the prisoners had become incapacitated at that range. Mike and Gabor had positioned themselves far enough away from the prisoners that this radio conversation could not be overheard and the prisoners would have no reason to fake collapse.

Even at half a mile range the effect was immediate, the fit highly trained soldiers became entirely immobilised instantaneously. It was decided to transport them to the crowded city of Puerto Quetzal, give them another dose a mile or two out of the city and then, whilst they were still confused and disorientated release them in the streets, there to be found by whomever, probably to be reported and eventually returned to the USA.

The conspirators returned to Naranjo when the job was complete, Julio put the equipment securely into hiding having removed all batteries to prevent leakage or decay and having wrapped everything and protected it from damp.

Mike opined that the trouble would stop now, but he wasn't confident. He knew the Yanks would want their kit back, he also knew they'd have no idea who had captured the Green Berets, but, if they found out he was anywhere in the locality...

David and Linda would have sailed south long ago, his passport was useless to all intents and purposes, he was reliant on Julio and Gabor to hide and protect him. He still had his thousand dollars with which to make a contribution, but even so it was not really any kind of permanent solution. Might provide time to think though and Julio could keep an eye on the news media at least. He longed to confer with Tanya. Dare he risk a phone call?

Eventually he could bear it no more and risked placing a call to Josey's landline. He got Josey, Tanya was at evening classes. Good and bad, he knew where Tanya was for certain and he knew that Josey and Monkey hadn't bought the idea that he was a maniacal killer, bad because he couldn't say much to Josey; he asked her to tell Tanya that he was safe, he was in Guatemala and enigmatically to say he'd learned something but he couldn't say what.

CHAPTER TWENTY ONE - HOBBS AND DONOHUE

"Two of our Green Berets got brought back from Guatemala today. From what appears to have gone on there I'll wager our boy is there, in Guatemala."

"You'd best explain"

"We had some Green Berets test this thing in a real life scenario down in Guatemala, works pretty good."

"What! You didn't think to tell us you were doing this? Unfucking believable. FUBAR in fact, are your people crazy?"

"It gets worse, or better, depending how you look at it, someone tipped the locals off as to what was happening as I see it, and as I see it there's only one person that could be."

"You don't think there could have been a leak, or someone saw something, or local helpers took a bribe?"

"Any of those things are possible but we have to send people down there to try and recover the kit and paper over the holes, I bet your so called taxi driver will show up. If he was in the States still we'd have him by now and if he's not how did he get out? I told you he's working for the Russians, the Chinese, North Korea, Iran, someone we don't get along with anyhow."

"You won't be getting along with your own bloody allies at this rate."

"That's above your pay grade. We're gonna get to the bottom of this. You and I are flying down tonight with some more of my old comrades unless you Brits are crying off."

"That too is above my pay grade, unless I'm taken off a job I see it through."

Donohue and Hobbs arrived in Guatemala with six Green Berets keen to recover the honour of their outfit and quite prepared to rough up, or worse, anyone who got in the way. Hobbs conferring with his superiors in the UK still expressed the view that O'Brien was just a nosey taxi driver in the wrong place at the wrong time, but admitted that if he turned out to be behind, or involved in recent events in Guatemala there would be an awful lot of explaining to do.

The entire operation in Guatemala, the sheer arrogance of it, ruffled feathers in Whitehall. "My god, bloody Lancaster" Dearlove muttered to himself. They themselves had let the cat out of the bag so it was hard if not impossible to complain, however they'd keep this as a bargaining chip for when they wanted something he suggested to Blair, who was himself as incredulous as he was powerless.

"Clinton would have seen heads roll for this, but now we have George W. Bush, I haven't met him yet, but we have spoken. Of course he's much to the right of Clinton, and myself frankly. They say he's not the sharpest knife in the drawer and some of the things he comes out with support that theory, but I think he's identified a type of voter that identifies with that, you know, any good ol' boy can become president idea. I think he plays on it, we'll see.

I'm going to have to continue to be America's best friend and pick only those battles we can win."

Lancaster had paid a high price, after losing his job and his pension and getting thrown out on his ear, he had something approaching a breakdown, when he tried to blame the whole thing on his wife, for shouting at him in the street she too sent him packing and divorced him.

The USA liked to appear as the world's policeman despite protestations to the contrary and they certainly didn't want to appear as a rogue state driving a coach and horses through international laws, conventions and norms. Blair could use that if and when the time came.

Tensions between the UK and the USA security services had also only heightened in the intervening period without success, or even much in the way of leads. Furthermore, the British security services who now had more people assigned to the task at home were not impressed that the Americans had trialled and risked their invention on innocent civilians in clear breach of their obligations under the UN charter and despite both nations having seats on the Security Council.

The British felt this thing needed to be kept under wraps until, and in case it was ever needed for a large battlefield deployment. Everyone felt Russia, for example, was neutered and the Russians didn't like to be so thought of. What if they invaded Europe for example?

This thing could stop an invasion in its tracks and yield up hundreds of thousands of uninjured and unarmed prisoners who would want to go home. Prisoners whose parents and wives, fiancées, grandparents and siblings would want them home, a huge bargaining chip. Not to mention all their hardware which would have been captured, could be studied and which, in being captured, would have severely depleted the other side's ability to wage war.

That the Americans had risked the surprise and all this, just in order to potentially move people around, for what, a silver mine, a coffee plantation! Then they'd gone and lost it, it kept on coming back to that though, the Yanks only have it because we lost it too.

In addition, on the American side a change of President heralded a change of foreign policy and the CIA wanted this thing put to bed before it became clear which way the wind was blowing.

In Guatemala it soon became evident that the original two Green Berets, now on what would turn out to be permanent leave had been a bit too enthusiastic and had been carried away with themselves. Of course Donohue and Hobbs and the mopping up operation knew where their boys had operated from and who their assistants were.

The helpers confirmed that Doug and Bruce had simply failed to turn up for their final mission and that until they'd heard that the two of them had been found wandering dazed and confused in the streets of Puerto Quetzal they'd just assumed they had everything they wanted and had decided to end the mission. After the news broke they knew something had gone wrong, but elected to keep their heads down and keep out of it.

That made sense, but it revealed nothing about who was behind the capture. Since Xinka settlements had been used for the trial it made sense to think that someone in the Xinka community had taken action.

The team of helpers the original Green Berets employed were Garifuna, a mix of indigenous people and descendants of African slaves originally from St Vincent. Despite not being Xinka they could travel around to trade without arousing suspicion. The four of them were recruited on increased pay to separately visit places such as Naranjo and the smaller settlements in Xinka territory to listen for information.

It wasn't long before word reached Hobbs and Donohue that there was a gringo with no obvious reason to be there, no business, no occupation, living in a small village a few miles from Naranjo.

In fact Julio and Gabor had sorted a home for Mike that was little more than a hut and where he was living alone. Julio's group of comrades met infrequently partly for security, but also because they all had a living to make one way or another. Julio had tasked a local villager to help Mike cope with life in the forest, to pass on any messages Mike might want to send him and of course to report if anything newsworthy occurred. He regarded Mike as a brother now, but there was only so much you could do. Mike would have to work out and find his own path, or stay and live in the forest, his call.

One morning Julio was awoken early by his friend from the village, he wasn't a young man and he was straining for breath.

"Sit down, drink. OK tell me."

"They have him, Mike, they came for him, he's gone."

"Who came?"

"Americans, Americans came, they took him, they were not kind, not gentle."

Julio thanked the man and made him rest and break fast before allowing him to return. He called a meeting of the comrades.

"Mike has been taken by the Americans, there is nothing we can do for him. They would love us to use the EDT, but they'd be ready with their headsets, there would be more of them than us, we don't know where they've taken him, he could be out of the country even now and if six of us with the helmets we can muster started a fire fight it would not end well for us I think.

"Mike is gone, we can't help him physically, I'll get a message to Felipe in America, he's made some contacts who may be in a position to help I think, that is all we can do for Mike.

"Now we have to think about ourselves. Mike will talk."

There was some shaking of heads.

"He will talk because they will make him talk, drugs, torture whatever they use they will get the information they want, they will be looking for us and they will be looking for it. They won't get it back, only I know where it is, if I think I'm going to die I will share that information only with Gabor.

"We have all lived as guerillas before and this is not a war as we knew it. The Americans have limited numbers here, they are not the government. It's not good, it's not nice, it's not convenient, it doesn't make me happy but we disappear, we disappear to the four corners of Guatemala if necessary. WE do not get caught. We meet here in one year."

Everyone nodded.

"Tell your families you have to go away for a while for the sake of our Xinka cause, do not give any details, let them know you are safe occasionally, use the methods we used before, do not let them know where you are. I think, I believe in one year the Americans will have given up, they will assume the batteries are dead, that it's no longer a threat and anyway the Americans have no staying power, we can fight for thirty six years!"

He raised his glass. "Comrades."

Within a couple of hours they had disappeared into thin air.

CHAPTER TWENTY TWO - REPORTERS

Washington Post reporter Daniel Koopmanns is on the horns of a dilemma. He's been approached by a disgraced Green Beret, who has hit the bottle and taken to gambling who wants to sell his story. Naturally he doesn't want to tell the story first, he wants money. Koopmanns offers him a thousand dollars to get the bones, the man calling himself Bruce laughs and demands ten thousand for a taster.

"It's huge, I'm telling you man, the biggest story of your career, I promise you, we can talk about a fee for the whole thing later."

"I can't advance ten thousand bucks to any, pardon me sir, drunken Joe that walks in here saying he's got the story of a lifetime! Koopmanns curiosity was piqued though and he would love to get something over on the military or the CIA. Fifteen hundred and it better be good, you leave me a number where I can get you and I talk to the editor, he will decide if we're interested and he will decide what it's worth, capische."

Bruce got his fifteen hundred and revealed he'd been sent to Central America, wouldn't say where, to test, on civilians no less, a new secret weapon that disabled people without killing them, enabling them to be relocated. He offered up the opinion that something corrupt was going on at the CIA and it was a dry run for clearing people from their lands for a silver mine. He didn't reveal he and his comrade had lost the damned thing, or any more details, he wanted a million.

Koopmanns took his details and showed him out. Experience of people suggested to him that, when Bruce had pissed the fifteen hundred up the wall, or gambled it away, or both he'd be back wanting to sell the next instalment and more desperate by then he'd give away the where and the how for probably another thousand. Before long Koopmanns would have the whole story. He just had to hope Brucie boy wasn't doing the rounds of all the papers! 'A million indeed, hah'.

Bruce meantime was already in a local bar celebrating the million bucks to come.'I served my country and this is how they treat me, I put my life on the line for them'.

"Give me the bottle, I'm celebrating."

Felipe had news from home. A man of his tribe had visited him at McDonalds, they had met after work and the man had gone again. Now, at last, Felipe had something interesting and concrete to tell Bill and Charlotte.

Naturally the CIA had been watching Felipe as they had been watching Bill and Charlotte and since Felipe was living with them he was under scrutiny too. Unfortunately the noisy bar prevented adequate recording, all they knew was that Felipe had held a long hushed discussion with a man who looked as if he too was from Guatemala. How that man had given them the slip when he left was an embarrassment. They couldn't take Felipe in because he was living with a lawyer and a journalist who'd be all over the case like a rash, probably already were.

"I have something important to tell you."

Bill shook his head and picked up a piece of paper, he wrote, not here, they can probably listen, Amnesty have security, we go to their office, now.

Felipe had an interesting story to tell. He explained that a man named Mike had turned up in Guatemala and had helped capture two Green Berets and a transmitter of some sort which incapacitated people plus six helmets that protected a person from the effects. Bill and Charlotte looked at one another, their eyes discussing whether to reveal that they knew this Mike. On a need to know basis they decided no. Felipe was more likely to be taken in on a trumped up charge and questioned than them.

Only Tanya was free and in the clear. Unwatched.

A lady checked into the Marriott Marquis and asked to have a meeting with the conferencing manager.

She began the conversation "Hello Tanya, how did you enjoy the Cher concert at Sturgis?"

She handed Tanya a letter from Charlotte, she didn't believe she'd been followed and she didn't believe the authorities were on to Tanya, nonetheless she told Tanya to read it and destroy it.

In the letter Charlotte said she desperately wanted the story herself but she couldn't risk Tanya's position being the only person able to operate unwatched. She suggested Tanya approach a credible paper with national distribution, maybe the Post or the Times. She was certain if she ran the story her editor would be told no way, national security, long before it hit the presses, because she herself was under such close scrutiny.

Bill thought that their home was bugged and Charlotte's office probably was too. He hoped they hadn't been able to do that at Amnesty but even there he wouldn't trust phones, even burner phones as they could monitor the signal from those if they knew the location.

Tanya immediately booked the next week off as leave and travelled to Washington DC where she obtained an appointment with Washington Post reporter John Roberts. She had no interest in money and had an incredible story to tell. John being young, and full of spunk as he saw it, was more interested in making eyes at Tanya than listening to her story. He mentally dismissed it out of hand as a fairy story, but he asked for her number and suggested that maybe they should go for a drink to talk about it. His attitude told Tanya all she needed to know.

"I came here to give you a story of national importance and all you want is to get in my pants, you can fuck right off."

That night, John went for a drink with his mentor at the paper, the far more experienced Daniel Koopmanns.

"Gorgeous girl in here today, complete nut job though, reckons she knows about a secret weapon the CIA are trying out in Guatemala, where the hell is some bimbo receptionist, or whatever she is, going to get a story like that?"

"Did you get her contact details?"

"No the bitch just swore at me and left, shame she was hot man, I mean real hot."

Daniel groaned and thought about telling John about his soldier. Thought better of it and decided that tomorrow a meeting with the editor was now called for. His evening went downhill after that.

The meeting with the editor didn't go down as well as Koopmanns might have wished either, he got on well with the boss, but he was cautious.

"One source ex military, we can't protect him and by talking he's in breach of the law, it seems there's another source, but we don't know who she is or where she came from, then there's the legal department, who will say, and quite rightly, that we can't go giving away national security secrets just to sell papers. There may be something here we can use, but you'd better find that girl and get her back here."

CHAPTER TWENTY THREE - THE CAT HAS NINE LIVES

Mike faced his interrogators, at least he knew who they were this time. Hobbs kept silent and appeared as an observer only, in order to hide the fact of his Britishness. Hobbs still felt instinctively, even now that O'Brien was not an agent of some foreign power, but he admitted even he needed a credible explanation in order to confirm that.

Donohue was equally convinced that they had finally captured an elusive foreign agent and he now wanted to get the handler and everyone else behind O'Brien's repeated miraculous escapes. He's not happy to have received instructions to go easy on O'Brien, no waterboarding, not even sleep deprivation and bright lights this time. Considering O'Brien had given sod all away at the first interrogation he was outraged and felt they should go much, much further this time. Human rights weren't high on Donohue's list of what really mattered in the world.

He would have been incandescent with rage had he known that his so called partner had gone behind his back and persuaded MI6 to urge Blair to take diplomatic steps to ensure a British subject he believed to be innocent was not tortured or harmed in any way.

Had Donohue known that time was limited and that steps were already being taken to return O'Brien to British jurisprudence, the initial accusation having originated on British soil and the accused himself being a British subject without any dual nationality, Donohue might have taken the law into his own hands and at least have given O'Brien the black eyes and broken teeth he felt the prisoner deserved. He really wanted to vent his fury for month, after month, after month of fruitless searching, a failure which embarrassed, frustrated and annoyed him greatly.

He could not understand that his partner, who should be equally embarrassed and at least as angry, given it was a British secret that had been leaked, should be so calm. In fact Hobbs had more in common with Bill Standing in that he cared more for the facts, logic, the rule of law and the outcome rather than merely his personal loss of face. He begrudgingly admired O'Brien as an adversary, even if he had had the apparatus of a foreign power behind him, if he did not, as Hobbs believed, how much more remarkable was it what O'Brien had so far accomplished. For two former special services soldiers the Hobbs and Donohue really had very little in common.

From O'Brien's perspective he knew that the game was now well and truly up and that for him it was make or break time. He could tell his story slowly, who knew what Tanya was up to, or Julio for that matter, but hoping for a miracle wasn't realistic. His aim was to get his life back, well, not the old one exactly, the life he dreamed of spending with Tanya, till death do us part. However, they were already parted and death seemed like a very possible outcome and not far off at that.

O'Brien's strategy was to go slowly, tell them things they already knew, in order to verify that he was telling the truth and then to dig his heels in and say he would only reveal the rest of his story to the British police or security services, his being a British subject.

So it began O'Brien talked about the fateful night he'd picked up James Lancaster, he explained about Lancaster's verbal fight with his wife and how in his haste to get indoors he left his tough-book or whatever they call that sort of laptop. He admitted he'd been wrong to tamper with it, of course he had no idea that Lancaster was MI5, he was just bored and nosey, wrong but it hardly warranted kidnapping, torture and a year on the run.

Anyway, yes he'd found out things he shouldn't have. At this juncture he claimed to be tired and hungry and said he was happy to continue his story, but only after a meal and they might do it in more comfortable surroundings, he was no flight risk, he wanted to clear his name.

Donohue was outraged that his superiors agreed, no good cop, bad cop, just good cop all the way! With tactics like these O'Brien dragged things out to the max but told the story of his escape from the kidnappers in great detail. He wanted to be scathing, sarcastic and contemptuous but he felt one of his questioners harboured a real hatred and he didn't want to inflame it. One of them had never opened his mouth, just jotted down notes despite the recording being made.

Nonetheless a discussion wasted time, he said he had now worked out that it wasn't Russians or anyone else that had kidnapped him, he knew it was the CIA, so how had they been so careless as to let him escape?

"You didn't escape, you were allowed to think you'd escaped, we put a tracker on you and anticipated you would lead us to your confederates."

"If I had a tracker on me how in god's name did I get away?"

"Luck, the tracker was in your shoe."

O'Brien didn't know whether to laugh or cry.

He didn't know how much they already knew, they must know about Dave Harrison's role, that much was apparent, but had they found out about Sarah? He suspected not. He continued with the story as far as reaching the home of his buddy then insisted he needed sleep and was amazed to find himself accommodated.

Next morning after a pretty decent breakfast he continued the story as far as borrowing Dave's passport and cards, borrowing his clothes too. At this point he insisted he be told what had happened to his friend, he swore his friend knew nothing about the secrets he'd uncovered.

Donohue's superior assured O'Brien that since Harrison believed he was protecting his friend from a foreign power or mafia organisation, and given that the security breach would be made far worse by a court case, it had been decided that charges were inappropriate. Harrison even had a new passport.

'Christ all bloody mighty, they're just chatting to him as if he was a friend' Donohue's thoughts were increasingly angry.

They reached the point where Mike flew to Canada, with plans to elude the Russians in some backwater in the USA when lunchtime came around.

After lunch Mike put his spanner in the works, he said he'd been honest but after everything that had happened to him, especially his first experience of CIA tactics he wanted to speak with the British Security Services, he was British, the secret device was British, he was stopping there.

Donohue was actually quite pleased, a refusal to cooperate would instigate far tougher measures he was certain. At which point his bloody partner opened his mouth.

"I'm here for MI6 Mike you can speak freely."

"And you are."

"Sean Hobbs I was assigned to find you alongside Donohue here."

Donohue was outraged to have been named but a hand on his shoulder from his superior shut his mouth even before he opened it.

"Pleased to meet you Mr Hobbs, you understand that staying alive is one of my main priorities, it's largely dictated every action I've taken, second to that is once again having a life, an identity, a job, maybe get married, you know, normal stuff. I don't think remaining in custody here in the USA is conducive to any of that."

"I can tell you that plans are already being made to transfer you to custody in London, but for all of us time is of the essence, the weapon you discovered could disarm an army in the field, it could prevent the invasion of Europe for example, it is imperative for the future security of all that it remains secret and that it remains only in the hands of Britain and the USA, even fellow NATO allies are unaware."

Mike felt a surge of anger for the first time.

"Then it was bloody stupid to go use it for some ethnic cleansing operation in Central America, you people make me sick."

Hobbs remained calm.

"I personally agree with you and that is being discussed at the very highest levels I assure you."

"So that was a purely American initiative I take it?"

"I cannot confirm or deny that, but we need to put a lid on this thing and we aim to recover our equipment."

"Well good luck with that one."

Mike realised he might be going too far.

"Look you're in a hurry and I'm more than willing to cooperate, given guarantees that I won't be prosecuted, I've suffered enough for hacking into a random laptop, I want my freedom, my passport and I want a life, possibly a new identity after being branded a serial killer. Give me that and I will tell you everything I know, all of it. London is only a few hours away by air, and if I'm on an RAF flight with UK personnel I'll start filling in what you don't know right away, as soon as we're in the air."

Hobbs turned to look at David Phelps, Donohue's boss at the CIA and Pentagon liaison with direct access to the President day and night. The most senior person in the room. Hobbs looked him straight in the eye and said nothing. Phelps blinked first.

"Very well I'll talk to the President, make your call Hobbs, if we're doing this your plane better be airborne within the hour."

Donohue spoke .

"I'll get ready."

"I think I'll take over from here Kevin, thank you for your contribution."

CHAPTER TWENTY FOUR - WHO GOES WHERE

Things started to happen at pace now. Tanya contacted Charlotte and told her of her experience at the Washington Post.

"Bloody fool, you got a junior no doubt, I don't know why I didn't think of this before, distance and cost I suppose, look, I've got a friend at The Independent in London, she thinks like Bill and me, cares about injustice, that kind of thing. Can you get to London? I can call her, we're getting through some bloody phones here I can tell you. Anyway I can forewarn her to take you seriously and I'm afraid I have some bad news, we just found out that Mike has been captured in Guatemala, he was helping local tribes people protect themselves.

Looks like our charming CIA have been trying this thing out down there. There are even rumours it was a precursor to clearing some forest for a silver mine or something. Anyway, your Mike was on the side of the angels but he got himself caught."

"Oh god Mike, what will they do to him?"

"Honestly Tanya I can't say, I'm so very sorry. Bill is working on it, he'll talk with Amnesty but these things take time, if the US government want Mike to disappear for good then I really fear for him. I think if we can make headway in Britain, I mean he's a British citizen right, if a story runs there he's no longer anonymous and forgotten, makes it harder to get rid of him, the Brits might want him back badly enough to actually dig their heels in, you never know. If you want to help Mike and of course I know you do, get yourself to London, here are the details."

Tanya found herself on the ubiquitous Boeing 747 Jumbo Jet flying to Heathrow whilst at the same time Mike was being routed to Brize Norton on an RAF Boeing Globemaster. Tanya spent her time worrying and feeling a mixture of fear and also excitement that she was finally doing something concrete to help.

Aboard Mike's flight were Sean Hobbs (who now took over the questioning), David Phelps, the flight crew, a catering detail and four RAF regiment bods, just in case the prisoner tried anything foolhardy. No one expected such a thing, the crew were briefed that a UK national was to be collected together with an MI6 officer and a high ranking CIA officer who was to be regarded as a VIP. Only the RAF regiment bods were aware that the civilian was technically a prisoner and that barring any kind of trouble he was not to be treated so much as a prisoner as a guest.

The soldiers were located out of earshot, catering came only when called. Mike continued with his story. He explained how he'd got to Lindsborg, the Greyhound buses the money, disposing of the credit cards and how he'd created a life there, he explained that he'd left when the missing persons circular reached the local sheriff, all very plausible as far as it went.

He failed to mention that Sarah had a missing husband, or that she was still in receipt of said husband's pension. He wasted more time by talking about Pop and Angie. Hobbs made a mental note to check up on this Sarah it seemed odd she'd been willing to hide a man and give him a truck to escape with, but, people have done stranger things. By going into great detail about unimportant matters Mike managed to drag it out so that they were on the ground before he got around to Tanya Brown.

From Brize Norton the group were whisked by road to the SIS Building at Vauxhall Cross where the questioning continued.

The story of course then became all about Tanya and Mike struggled in the telling. He could hardly deny knowing her surname. Fortunately, having described his time with Sarah in great detail, apart from the obvious omission, he actually delayed mention of Tanya until she was safely on the ground in Heathrow, a stroke of great good fortune he knew nothing about, since Phelps immediately requested information on both Sarah and Tanya and their respective families and friends, and as an extra precaution their details were put on the system to flag them up if they attempted to leave the country.

In the event it threw up that Tanya Brown was already out of the country and in the UK. That certainly had to be more than mere coincidence. Mike of course was oblivious that his constant prevarications had allowed her to take action on his behalf.

He drew the narrative out further by describing Sturgis and the subsequent road trip in far greater detail than necessary. Finally he expressed his disgust at being labelled a serial killer and described how he got out of that fix. The CIA were quickly able to ascertain that yacht Allegria had sailed from San Francisco on the appropriate date. Everything had a ring of truth about it.

Tanya had a meeting scheduled with Charlotte's friend Rosie Osborn a political journalist at The Independent. It was a long one. She started by saying that her boyfriend was British and a prisoner of the CIA, that he had accidentally discovered information with a bearing on national security and that she believed his life was in danger.

"That's why I'm here, but it's a long story, first I'll explain how I met Mike. Then I'll tell you most of what he told me, then I'll tell you how he escaped from the USA, only to be picked up in Guatemala where the CIA were carrying out attacks on civilians in violation of international law, and then, and then I don't know. Charlotte told me Mike had been picked up, it's not public knowledge by any means."

Ordinarily Rosie would have been very sceptical, but unlike the young reporter at the Post who thought with the apparatus below his waist Rosie knew from long experience that strange things happen, especially when it comes to governments, conflict, espionage, terrorism; she had an open mind and she'd been told in no uncertain terms by her friend and fellow liberal Charlotte to take this thing seriously.

Some two hours later when Tanya was winding up her account, despite numerous interruptions, questions and clarifications all doubts were erased when Rosie's assistant entered the room and said "I think you should know there's a guy called Koopmanns on the phone from the Washington Post wanting to know if anyone here has been approached by a lady called Tanya."

"Well something has made them think again, I wonder what they know? Desperate stuff to call the competition. They'll probably suggest working on it together, pooling resources and information, but I think we probably know enough already without them. Although clearly they've picked something up.

"The Post won't be the only people looking for you, you know that, depending how long he's been in custody Mike has almost certainly revealed your name by now. Don't look so disbelieving, he has no choice, they won't let him escape again, if push comes to shove these people can be very nasty, they call it persuasive but believe me it's nasty, and the final thing is that Mike will want what they can offer, his freedom, if he loves you as much as you seem to love him, he'll be desperate to get himself in the clear, even if it takes a few years in jail to do it.

"If he's smart he'll tell them everything but let it out as slowly as possible to buy time, he's not without friends on the outside, even if he doesn't know what his friends are doing on his behalf. A story like this requires a meeting not just with the editor, but also with legal. I've got about three hours of recordings here, even if I précis it for the meeting it'll be another long one and it won't happen before tomorrow morning now, even if the editor is working late legal will have gone home. I'll make some calls and get it set up for as early as possible, maybe seven in the morning with bacon sarnies, tea and croissants. You OK with that?"

Tanya nodded.

"I strongly suggest you spend the night on a camp bed here, you can't check into a hotel, they'll sweep you up in an instant. They'll suspect you've gone to one of the papers but they won't know which one, plus they'll be busy checking who you are, who your family are, whether you're some kind of dissident or trouble maker. They'll be very busy right now and they don't raid newspaper offices without a warrant, it's bad publicity! So, we have just enough time to make our plans, it's a camp bed for you and a pizza if you know what's good for you. Actually it's a camp bed and a pizza for both of us, I can't go home and leave you wandering around here."

While Tanya bedded down in the newspaper office Hobbs was back on a return flight across the Atlantic to talk with Sarah, it was felt that, being English, he could pose as a friend of Mike's, Dave Harrison even. Sarah may well remember the name and might have forgotten the passport photo even if she'd seen it, it seemed likely that Sean Hobbs who appeared to have a gift for police work could confirm what O'Brien had told them. Any holes in his story whatsoever would change the picture entirely.

Tanya Brown was more of a problem, since, whilst she was probably in London so were about seven million other people, hotels were being advised of the name, police had been given the name and a picture, out of date, from a school yearbook, but a picture nonetheless, they'd try to get a newer one but by all accounts so far she hadn't changed much. Eventually they tied her to the Guatemala demonstration, they had a recent picture now too, but too late. By then Tanya had not only told her story to Rosie but also to the editor and the barrister employed by the Independent for such sticky matters.

At around ten thirty that morning the Independent decided to call the Ministry Of Defence with the bones of the story they proposed running and request a comment or denial in order to test the water. Within forty minutes an injunction signed by a judge was delivered by courier, something of a record and as if he'd been waiting, which he had in fact, a minute later an MI5 officer had presented his credentials and a warrant to take away any and all evidence pertaining to the case.

The Independent complied but were not a complete pushover, they handed over the tapes, they had copies anyway, and they hid Tanya who they claimed had left in the night. Hobbs was well on his way to Lindsborg and Bill and Charlotte were boarding a flight to London with Felipe.

CHAPTER TWENTY FIVE - NO LOOSE ENDS

Amnesty International were making waves. They claimed knowledge that a London taxi driver was being held without trial and claimed that International Law had been broken in Guatemala, that the two cases were linked and that they wanted to see Mike O'Brien released unharmed.

Headquartered in London, Amnesty founder Peter Benenson was a lawyer who'd made his name helping political prisoners. This could be said to be Amnesty's specialist subject, they'd contacted the UK foreign office and now that Bill Standing and key witness Felipe were in London they'd also contacted the US Embassy demanding information.

The Americans were able to say that they had picked up a British National on suspicion of espionage in Guatemala and that they had, naturally returned him to the British authorities for questioning. They could not comment on potential crimes in Guatemala without further information.

Even MI6 realised they couldn't hold Mike O'Brien indefinitely without charges given outsiders knew they had him, that despite some leeway being afforded SIS there were limits. A crisis meeting was held at the Foreign Office. Amnesty brought Bill Standing, one of their own UK lawyers and Felipe as a witness. Somehow they'd found Tanya Brown before the British police too. Charlotte as a foreign journalist was persona non grata, as was any journalist from the Independent however the Independent's barrister was present.

For the Foreign Office no less a person than Jack Straw the Foreign Secretary, a British Government minister was in attendance, a senior representative of MI5 who had started this whole thing, Sir Stephen Lander, embarrassed, had sent a deputy, but his organisation having been the most involved Sir Richard Dearlove attended in person. David Phelps represented the CIA and the US Ambassador to the UK William Stamps Farrish III was also in the room.

It was an unprecedented collection of individuals a genuine David and Goliath meeting. If Tanya's folks could see her now! That was not her concern though. The presence of such high ranking individuals was not primarily intended to intimidate, although in particular it did intimidate Tanya and Felipe very considerably, the Amnesty representative and the lawyers were not intimidated and Mike had been through so much he hardly cared any more, just wanted it over, whatever the outcome, although he knew very well what his preferred outcome would be.

No, the reason these people were here was to make definite decisions and wind this thing up satisfactorily before anything else went wrong. Any decision reached at the meeting which met with the approval of the Foreign Secretary and David Phelps would be rubber stamped by both the Prime Minister and The President. Both knew what they could and could not accept.

Mike testified to having been kidnapped by the CIA posing as agents of a different power after he hacked into a compute left in the back of his taxi. Everyone was well briefed, so the whys and wherefores of the computer being left in the cab and how Mike had obtained the information to hack it were already well known to the British team and the Ambassador.

What they wanted to know was how much did other people know about the technology. Felipe understood that it disabled people and that a helmet of some sort offered protection, he clearly did not understand how, or what the technology was, or how it worked., of course it wasn't going to be certain how much Mike had revealed to other people but without illegal means of interrogation they'd pretty much have to take things at face value, it appeared as if no one knew how it worked except Mike. He confirmed he'd kept as much to himself as possible in order to protect his friends.

That left the missing transmitter and headsets in the helmets. Felipe confirmed that his friends in Guatemala had realised they could not use the device without causing waves and repercussions which would bring retribution down on their heads and that they'd had enough of war, they just wanted to live in peace, so they'd buried the stuff in the forest and gone into hiding.

He did not say that the batteries had been removed and that everything had been carefully protected and placed in a pre prepared weapons store, he just gave the impression that a large hole had been dug and everything thrown in with the earth heaped on top.

The security people confirmed that the batteries would have a limited life, that after a few months in the ground corrosion would have done its worst and that if anyone did dig it up they wouldn't know what they were looking at.

It was far from ideal, but the chances of finding it were about one in a hundred million, even with metal detectors, or helicopter or drone flights over the forest, with LIDAR or ground penetrating radar. The forest was too vast, the trees too dense.

It transpired then that Mike was the one and only real risk, as they saw things, still the loose cannon who knew too much. However, what were they to do with him, he was still a British citizen with rights, he hadn't disappeared, plenty of people knew he was alive, he had Amnesty International and both British and American lawyers in his camp. Furthermore some idiot had thought it a smart idea to libel him and claim he was serial killer, if he brought the legal cases his American lawyer threatened in the States then that would be a story that could not be subject to an injunction in the UK, it simply wouldn't stand up.

Straw offered a compromise.

"If the British government pays compensation in place of the, compensation he'd get from the American media then that prevents a media circus and the story of the computer in the cab, the weapon wrongdoing in Guatemala, that all goes away, remains subject to injunctions on both sides of the Atlantic

"William, your people put that story out if we agree compensation you're paying half, the Ambassador nodded, enough between a politician and an Ambassador.

"Mr Standing, I'm doing you out of work here, but it's in the interests of your country as well as ours. What I'm proposing is that O'Brien here signs the official secrets act, we'll throw the book at him if he talks, he'll never see the outside of a prison again, but if he signs and accepts the compensation then it's immediate, no waiting for the American courts, no long drawn out hearings, I can transfer funds today and he's free to go. How much would Mr O'Brien get in the USA?"

"For libel like that, from half the papers and TV Companies in the US I could see it reaching a hundred million dollars."

"You'd have to sue them all individually though I take, it so costs would be high I imagine?"

"That's true, but we'd likely get costs awarded."

"Someone would have to put a lot money up in the first instance to get the ball rolling would they not?"

"Yes."

"You?"

Bill looked doubtful.

"Can I say something? I'm not a greedy man, I just want to have a life, god knows what's happened to my home, I've got no money, I've been on the run for what, a year and a half, more. I've been tortured, threatened, chased from pillar to post, I want enough to get my life back on track and to not worry about money again.

A couple of million pounds would do it, one from the British government and one from the Americans, that and my freedom. That's chicken feed for you but Tanya and I can get married, build a new life somewhere, anywhere, we don't want to expose secrets or live in fear. Two million pounds, I sign on the line and the nightmare is over, agreed?"

"I can agree that. Agreed with you too William?"

"Yes, I'm authorised to agree that."

And just like that the meeting broke up. The money was transferred to Amnesty, that covered the government, it not being paid to an individual, which would be hard to account for. It also allowed Mike time to set up a new bank account, decide what he wanted to do about the house in Romford that kind of thing. In the interim Amnesty offered to advance Mike a large sum in cash so he could get a hotel and start to do things.

"You know what make an international transfer to the person I love most in the world, the person I trust most in the world and she can pay for the hotel on a card."

"Was that a proposal back there?"

"You're damn right it was; the toughest thing about sailing away, Guatemala, getting captured, didn't matter, the toughest thing was being separated from you."

Bill, Charlotte, Mike and Tanya checked into the Dorchester on Park Lane for a week, Mike showed them around the city he knew so well as a taxi driver, but eventually Bill and Charlotte had to return. Mike and Tanya had to make plans.

Over in America there were those in the CIA not happy with the outcome. Donohue especially.

"OK it wasn't all his fault I accept that now, he wasn't working for anyone else, OK, but if he hadn't been so bloody nosey, and he's still a security risk, OK he signed a bloody form, even so, he should have been dealt with."

His friends at the CIA knew what Donohue meant by 'dealt with', but they had their own jobs and cases to get on with and anyway Donohue wasn't Tenet's blue eyed boy any more.

Over in the UK Mike and Tanya very publicly bought a forty four foot Beneteau sloop, second hand, but still in the six figure price range and registered it in Mike's name. Even though Mike had been taught absolutely all he needed to know by David and Linda, certainly far more than was covered in a Day Skipper Course, nonetheless he and Tanya took the RYA Competent Crew and Day Skipper courses as well as the radio course, radar course, first aid and sea survival courses.

This they judged, with Mike's experience was plenty, they enjoyed doing them as a legitimate couple at last and it got them each an International Certificate of Competence recognised in many other countries. They managed to complete all these tasks before 2002 passed away.

Relaxed now they spoke freely to people they met in the marina about their plans to circumnavigate the globe using the Straits Of Magellan and Cape Horn with stops in places of interest all around the globe. It would be a ten year voyage of discovery, maybe longer, but first a wedding.

Tanya's folks would come to them, both felt it inadvisable to visit the USA just yet. The wedding took place in May of 2003. After the wedding they prepared their new boat, having the life raft serviced, registering their EPIRB, buying new distress flares, fitting a man overboard recovery system and danbuoy, solar panels and a wind generator were fitted to keep them powered up during long periods away from land.

Eventually, in the summer of 2003 they set sail from Falmouth in the Lady Tanya heading for The Isles Of Scilly and then The Canaries, Cap Verde, the Caribbean and thence down to South America via the Atlantic coast of Guatemala, to The Straits that would see them emerge on the Pacific side of Cape Horn without quite rounding the horn itself.

The world was literally their oyster, the major part of the money was invested for income although Bill, Charlotte, Josey, Monkey and Sarah had all received generous gifts. Liquid funds were invested in a joint account with Deutsch Bank as they had branches in very many countries. The wind was set fair. They departed on July 4th a day Tanya thought would be an auspicious one to begin their new life. Independence Day.

About three hundred yards out from Falmouth harbour a huge explosion ripped through the Lady Tanya, one second she was there, the next a few scraps of burning fabric and shards of rapidly disappearing fibreglass was all that anyone might see, within a minute or two, not even that.

It made the papers of course. Over in the USA Donohue opined that maybe the Limeys weren't as stupid as he'd thought. In the corridors of Whitehall and in the SIS building people cursed the Americans for always having to have the last word. No one claimed responsibility. The boat had been carrying a lot of cooking gas for such a long voyage, an investigation would reveal virtually nothing except the lead ballast from the keel. The destruction had been complete.

CHAPTER TWENTY SIX - THE ITALIAN JOB

In May 2005 an unusual event took place in the small southern Italian town of Benevento. It was hardly the crime capital of Southern Italy and although the Ndrangheta, Italy's most notorious Mafia organisation did operate in the south this event represented a new phase of operations. At least that was the worry for Police Inspector Massimo Capolupo.

On Tuesday the 3rd of May Deutsche Bank had been comprehensively robbed, several hundred thousand Euros in used notes had been taken. The attack took place just before opening time as staff entered the building and turned off the alarms, did their checks, took cash from the vaults to stock the tills. The streets were deserted.

Inspector Capolupo began by interviewing the staff, it was as if they'd made a pact to say nothing, not one of them was able to remember a thing about it. No matter he cajoled, threatened, not a one would move from that position. Eventually he gave up, there was no CCTV it wasn't really considered necessary in Benevento, Naples maybe, Reggio, but not Benevento.

"Oh well, he said to his assistant, I suppose one can't blame them for not wanting to testify, even judges have been killed, what chance do ordinary citizens stand, I might lose my memory myself rather than testify against the Ndrangheta"

EPILOGUE

In 2002 whilst Mike and Tanya were boat hunting in southern England and taking courses in Dartmouth another man was also looking for a boat. His name was Martin Addison and he'd come down from Glasgow and he spent several months in a hotel.

He was looking for something quite different from the sloop purchased by Mike and Tanya; he told brokers he was looking for a tough steel ketch, preferably a cutter ketch with a wheelhouse, long keel, relatively shallow draft and not very tall masts. A boat that could cross oceans, probably survive floating container strikes, but which could explore rivers, he meant the Rio Dulce, but he didn't say so.

He found what he was looking for and changed the name of the boat from the commonplace Carpe Diem to La Scappatella and registered her on the small ships register. He also purchased two complete sets of scuba gear. The only diving equipment Mike and Tanya carried were a couple of pony bottles and fins.

Addison was also preparing for a long voyage, his boat too had solar panels and a wind generator, a new life raft, an EPIRB registered in his name, which he sincerely hoped would never be needed, and a tender known as a Walker Bay which could be sailed, or motored with an outboard, or rowed.

Likewise Addison provisioned his boat for a long voyage and had a Danbuoy, life jackets, flares, grab bags, gybe controller. It was the perfect small, tough yacht for long distance, short handed sailing, no bells and whistles, not fast like a Beneteau but a real, go anywhere boat.

In June 2003 Addison moved his boat to the moorings outside Falmouth Haven yacht harbour and was frequently seen going about in his Walker Bay. Towards Dusk on July 3rd Addison motored away from La Scappatella in his dinghy with two sets of scuba gear minus fins.

When he returned to his boat the diving gear was no longer there. He hid the boat keys in the wheelhouse, hung the Walker Bay on the yacht's davits and secured it, mounted the outboard on the yacht's pushpit and padlocked it in place.

Finally he used his cellphone to call a water taxi to take him to the shore. Next day he was home in Glasgow, fingers crossed.

DISCLAIMER

This is my first novel, it is entirely fictitious, the premise of the story should really make that clear. All the major characters are fictitious and any resemblance to any person living or dead is entirely coincidental.

The names of almost all the characters and certainly all the main characters have been chosen by me almost at random. To make the story work I have used the real names of certain politicians who were in office at the time these fictitious events are supposed to have taken place. I have also used the real names of the heads of the security services in the UK and USA at that time.

I have never met any of these people, just as the novel is fictitious so are the characterisations and conversations. I'm making no comment whatsoever about the political policies pursued by the politicians at the time, nor am I passing any comment on how the security services were run, nor upon the leadership or style of leadership therein.

It's simply an adventure yarn. I hope a few people at least derive some pleasure from it. I'm not expecting a movie or a theme park, but I wouldn't say no!

Glossary

MILF - Mum I'd Like To Fuck.

FUBAR - military slang for Fucked Up Beyond All Recognition.

La Scappatella – The Escapade.

Pony Bottle, - A very small diving bottle and regulator holding enough air to possibly help out in an emergency or make a very short dive.

Acknowledgements

In my heart at least I would like to thank Kathy Rohn, for encouraging me to write down the story I carried in my head. That I failed to finish in Kathy's lifetime is my abject failure. I hope her husband, my friend Wolfgang, will enjoy the book.

It was pretty much a one man project, right down to the cover design I struggled with for days. All mistakes are mine and mine alone.

However, there would have been far, far more errors were it not for one particular buddy, and I wish to thank my good friend Amanda Kenny for hours and hours of copy checking and discussions by phone, which have certainly improved the end product markedly.

Thanks Amanda x

Copyright ©Malcolm Snook 2007

Printed in Great Britain
by Amazon